FACTS ABOUT HYDRAS

DR. RYAN K. STRADER

Clovercroft Publishing

Facts About Hydras

©2020 by Dr. Ryan K. Strader

Published by Clovercroft Publishing, Franklin, Tennessee

Edited by Gail Fallen

Cover and Interior Design by Suzanne Lawing

Printed in the United States of America

978-1-950892-16-7

"There will always be evidence, and every month fresh evidence, to show that religion is only psychological, justice only self-protection, politics only economics, love only lust, and thought itself only cerebral biochemistry."

—C.S. Lewis, *The Weight of Glory*

O Lord, I have a wild heart, and cannot stand before thee. I am like a bird before a man.

—*The Valley of Vision*

Everything everyone says makes perfect sense to them. Everything everyone believes makes perfect sense to them.

—From the hydra's journal

CONTENTS

FACTS ABOUT HYDRAS: PROLOGUE

The hydra sat patiently in the chair opposite the editor's desk. He had walked in, plunked the manuscript down on the desk, and was now paging through it as if he couldn't remember it and needed reminding. His eyes flicked up periodically to the hydra, trying to rationalize the red eyes and the spines and the way the hydra moved her legs constantly, trying to cross them and having difficulty. Human clothes were always too tight somewhere, and whenever the editor looked at her, she wished for the company of her missing heads.

"I mean, it's a very *strange* book," the editor finally said, leaning forward slightly and tapping the pages with his fingertips. "We haven't really published anything—um, well, with someone . . ." his voice trailed off.

"With a hydra?" the hydra asked helpfully.

"Yes," said the editor, relieved that this hydra was flippant. Who knew what other versions hydras might come in? At least with this one, he could be plainspoken. "And, I mean, it's confusing sometimes in the book, because, well, you know we are a Christian press and there are really some very big issues here."

"Well, I had to let my other heads talk a bit," said the hydra.

"Otherwise, it wouldn't be clear, you know, what it's like to be a hydra."

The editor blinked. "The other heads."

"Yes, hydras usually have more than one," the hydra said patiently. "That's what makes us hydras."

The editor continued to blink.

"More than one head," prompted the hydra. "That's what a hydra *is*."

"Yes, but . . . you have one," observed the editor.

"Oh, of course," nodded the hydra. "My others were cut off."

"Cut *off*?" sputtered the editor with a slight barking sound, like maybe it was funny or maybe his stomach hurt.

The hydra looked at him archly. She opened her messenger bag (larger than usual, because hydras are larger and tend to carry too many books) and out of its depths pulled a huge graying (it used to be green) head with a long floppy neck dangling from it. She held it up by the spines on top of the head, shaking out the neck a bit.

"They get wrinkled when I carry them around," muttered the hydra, shaking harder. A few tendons flipped out over the gasping editor's desk.

"So this one," said the hydra, breathless from shaking the long neck and putting on her teacher's voice, "this one was actually my second one that grew. This one never believed in God . . . or in anything, for that matter."

The hydra threw the floppy gray head onto the desk, and the editor pushed his chair back against the wall. Much to his dismay, the hydra pulled another head out of her bag and began to "shake the wrinkles" out of this one as well.

"I had this one much longer than the other one," said the hydra. "I'm not sure what this one believed, because she always changed the subject when asked a question."

The editor gulped. He pointed at the hydra. "And . . . the head you have now?"

The hydra sighed. "Did you read my manuscript? This is the only one I have now."

"But you used to have all three at once?" asked the editor.

The hydra pressed her shiny lips together and seemed to cross her short little reptilian arms. "If I had only ever had one head, I would just be a regular dragon. But I'm a hydra."

"Yes, I understand," said the editor, as if he were suddenly coming to. "But, my dear, hydras grow more heads when one is cut off."

"That's only in stories," said the hydra. "You're a grown man. Please tell me you know the difference between a story and a fact."

That silenced the editor for a few seconds.

"And anyway," continued the hydra, when it seemed the editor was not going to say something again right away, "that is only when someone *else* cuts off their head."

"What on earth do you mean?" asked the editor. "Who cut off your, your—" He waved his hands over his desk, motioning to the two floppy heads strewn across his desk.

"Well, I cut them off myself," admitted the hydra, seeming somewhat somber for a moment. "It was kind of unfortunate, because, you know, it hurt. But really, such things are inevitable."

"What in God's name are you talking about?" stuttered the editor. "Christians don't behead hydras. That's a Greek myth!"

The hydra narrowed her eyes and pressed her lips together again. The editor couldn't be sure, but he thought he saw the tiniest wisp of smoke curl out of one nostril.

"You didn't read the manuscript," she said accusingly. "It's not like some *other* Christian did it to me. I did it myself. And if I'm a myth, how am I sitting here in front of you?"

"I don't know," said the editor tightly. "But if you could please move these things off of my desk and collect your papers—" He moved his hand awfully close to the slack mouth of a decapitated head, and the mouth actually snapped at him.

"Be careful," said the hydra mildly. "They can still bite after they're dead. Similar to the way that dead wasps can sting."

"Well, I suggest you mention that in your revisions of the manuscript," suggested the editor fussily as the hydra carefully folded up the heads and stuffed them back in her bag. The editor slid the pages of the manuscript together and handed them to the hydra. "And then take it somewhere that they—ah—like to publish this sort of thing."

"And where might that be?" inquired the hydra curiously. "Do you know of a press that publishes work by hydras?" The hydra couldn't help but let a note of hopefulness into her voice. If there was a press that published work by other hydras, maybe they had hydra socials and whatnot.

The editor tried to think about it, but found it was very hard to consider the question. "I have no idea," he finally said in a defeated tone.

The hydra looked thoughtful. "But I really was hoping for a wider audience, you know."

"Nobody believes in hydras though," said the editor, taking a handkerchief out of his pocket and mopping his forehead. "I'm afraid that it's very hard to convince people that such a thing exists."

"I don't need to convince them. I'm standing right here," said the hydra.

"Yes, I see that," said the editor wearily.

"Maybe people just don't know," said the hydra. "Maybe they don't realize that I'm here, and I'm real."

The editor nodded. "I daresay they don't."

CHAPTER ONE

LESSON 1: INTRODUCTION TO THE WRITING PROCESS.

Good morning, class. Today's objective is to consider our pre-conceptions about the process of writing a paper. Or the process of writing anything, for that matter.

An effective process is not always linear. This is true about everything in life, and it's also true about writing a paper. This semester we will talk about the principles that you should keep in mind while developing your own process and approach to writing.

Being bogged down by imagined requirements for some set-in-stone writing process can make it difficult for you to write. Writing is hard enough, and some of your assignments in college will be hard enough, without you placing excessive pressure on yourself to draft in a certain way. Being flexible with your approach to your own process is far better for you because it will allow you to solve a wider array of writing problems more effectively.

Writing is an act of figuring something out, and such a process is rarely orderly. Sometimes you outline, sometimes you just spit out a draft. Sometimes you scrap that draft and start over, this time with an outline. Sometimes you outline by drafting. Sometimes a paragraph comes out lovely and orderly the first time, and then, strangely, you end up deciding that that same lovely paragraph just doesn't go in this piece of writing. So much for your earlier feeling of accomplishment. That magical little paragraph-sized package of sentences gets dropped in the trash. You can't get better at writing if you expect a canned, orderly process to work perfectly every time. You have to be willing to experiment, to throw stuff out, to start over.

When I was writing this book for you, I wrote the first eighty pages and had a pile of perfect shit on my screen. That is a true statement. It took me eighty pages to figure out what I was actually trying to say to you. So after eighty pages, I started over, on page one, with a clear vision for what I needed to tell you. But it took eighty pages to get there, to come back to that first page again.

Don't let that be discouraging. I often tell you that writing is like life. I say that because it's true. Many times in life you will get deep into something and say to yourself, "This is perfect shit. What have I done?" Time to revise. Or maybe just throw the whole pile out and start over.

You know, if writing were easy, everyone would do it. But they don't. Doing life well is also hard. I want you to be prepared.

That's why everyone should take a writing class. It teaches you how to think. It teaches you how to say, "Some of my preconceptions . . . well, they're shit."

* * *

This book is a fictionalized account of a real conversion, populated by mythical animals and lovable (and obnoxious) Christian students. Stylistically, it's a monster of a book. You may cite it in your papers, but only if you spell my name correctly. Which, none of you do.

I always tell you to be brief and "cogent" when you provide background material, so I'll do my best to be brief about my own background. Most of you know pieces of it already.

I spent my undergraduate years—all nine of them—at a large research school in the DC area. It was the late '90s. I was a product of '90s movies, television shows, and popular novels. As a comparative literature fiend, I studied several languages, took critical theory classes and loved cultural studies. I enjoyed being a feminist, a progressive who believed that the self is socially constructed. I started an activist newspaper on campus and worked my way through an awesomely liberal education.

In 2013 I arrived in a small Georgia town, much to my surprise and chagrin. My husband's job brought us down south, to the land of sunshine, churches, and squirrels. I got a job teaching writing and research methods at a small satellite campus of a larger university. Not only was I teaching writing out in the sticks of the Bible Belt, but I was also working on my doctorate at a university two hours away in a huge metropolitan city.

For several years, I divided my time between these two worlds: a woodsy campus under the sunny Georgia sky with students for whom church was the center of their social world, and a busy cosmopolitan campus located in a conglomeration of towers overlooking one of the busiest cities in the South.

I often tell you all how much I like teaching and that I

particularly like to teach writing. I do like to teach, in part, because I've always been good at it. I have always known that part of what makes me a good teacher is my view of my students. I value them. I think of every single one of them as their own essential little world, their own microcosm of interesting and complex thoughts. It's an essentialist view that I always knew was at odds with other parts of my materialist philosophy, but I was always a philosophical dilettante who enjoyed mixing perspectives. Contradictory stuff didn't bother me. Postmodernism is tolerant of contradiction: it just warmly wraps all the contradictions up in its big paws and hugs all the frustration away with a big relativistic squeeze. I loved the relative squeeze. I could feel all the annoyance and sense of logical disjunction just melt away when I imagined the postmodern squeeze.

From my first year teaching, I knew that, as far as a profession was concerned, I had found my home. I always thrived when I could teach, and my intrapersonal life usually took a nosedive when I was out of the classroom for a long period.

So, out in the sticks with the churches, I found a classroom and headed to my first day of freshman composition. I was excited to meet all of you, my students.

I'm not sure why it hadn't occurred to me that, since I was now living out in the sticks in a conservative area, that my students might not be exactly what I had been used to.

A common question for me to ask students during the first week of classes is, "What is the last really good book you read?" Students usually name something they read in their high school curriculum, so it gives me a sense of where my freshmen are coming from—did they all come from some place where they were forced to spend six months analyzing

The Scarlet Letter and now they're convinced that English teachers are morons? Did they come from a school that only assigns graphic novels?

On this particular day, the first four kids said, "The Bible."

Oh. "Are you all in Bible study together or something?" I quipped. Then I laughed . . . by myself.

The next kid also said, "The Bible."

Then a kid claimed that he didn't like to read. So he didn't have a book to name. I asked what he had read in high school.

He laughed and said, "Well, I went to a church school . . . and we were supposed to read the Bible sometimes . . . but I didn't." He stretched his arms out, like he might be stretching or he might be getting ready to hug somebody. "I really don't read books. Just being honest."

I decided right away I liked him. (I still liked him a few months later when he failed the class, don't worry.)

I decided to jump in and change the rules for a minute. "Okay, I realize that most of you are from communities where you read the Bible *a lot*," I said. "But I'm asking about what *other* books you have read, because I'm trying to learn *other things* about you. What kind of stories you enjoy, what kind of writing you have read and identified with. Let's start over, and name the last book you read that *wasn't* the Bible."

I kid you not, several students exchanged meaningful glances. Raised their little eyebrows at each other. Gave each other looks that were clearly a Liberal College Professor Alert. Then they turned back to me and obediently offered me non-Bible titles.

Interestingly, half of them named books from the Harry Potter series.

All right then, I thought happily. We all have the universe of Hogwarts in common, even if we have nothing else—like reality—in common. I might not be able to make lots of biblical analogies during lessons, but I can make a lot of Potter ones. And, I had learned that while many of them were conservative Christians, they weren't the book-burning kind. So far, so good.

Another thing I tend to ask students about within the first week of class is their news-reading habits: Where do they get the news from, and do they feel like they know and understand things that are going on in the world right now? This helps me get a handle on what kind of research topics might work for particular students, and what kind of extra reading I should assign. Needless to say, none of these kids read *The Wall Street Journal* or *The Washington Post* (my favorites) with great regularity.

On this particular first week of classes, a violent event perpetrated by an Islamic militant had put the concept of terrorism front and center in the news for the week. In asking students about their opinion on the event (which many of them hadn't heard about), I made the grave error of referring to "terrorism" as something that could come from any religious group. I was referencing terrorism in general and said some phrase like, "With any terrorist, if they are Muslim, or Christian—"

"There aren't Christian terrorists," harrumphed one kid.

"There can be terrorists who are Christians," I said, mentioning Timothy McVeigh and Anders Breivik as a couple of examples.

"Breivik never claimed to be a Christian," another student announced immediately. "His family was Christian, but he said he was never a Christian."

"And he isn't a Christian even if he says he is," explained another student.

Oh. That clarifies things.

The students were actually correct about Breivik, a fact I found interesting because it meant they knew why certain terrorists weren't Christian even though they didn't actually follow the current news and knew nothing about recent Islamic terrorist attacks.

"You mean that a Christian who was a terrorist would be interpreting Christianity or practicing it in a different way than you do. But he would still consider himself a Christian and be a Christian," I explained.

"No, he's not a Christian," said the kid with a shrug.

The next class, that same kid strode in. "I checked with my dad," he said. "And he says there's nothing in the Bible that justifies terrorism for a Christian. So that guy was not a Christian."

And this was just the first week. This was just my *introduction* to you kids.

* * *

The argument about Christian terrorists would resurface, as would debates about marriage and gender. I always tried to take the open-minded route. Since I thought of myself as a true progressive, I wanted to make space for everyone's ideas in the classroom. Everybody was welcome. Even when students had such intense convictions that they made it hard for me to be accommodating, I tried.

I believe that part of my job as an instructor is to give all students—regardless of their convictions—more language and more communication techniques than they had before entering the class. First-year writing classes are ostensibly offered because they give students the writing skills they need to be successful in their university endeavors, but I have always taught with the assumption that writing is about thinking and that the same thinking strategies that enable someone to write effectively are the same strategies that enable you to navigate life. The same thinking strategies that go into evaluating research and structuring a written argument are the same strategies that help someone to deal with conflict in the workplace or make parenting decisions. You have all heard me say that in class many times.

Not that you always remember.

The interesting thing about my approach to teaching at that time, though, was that I tried to coach you kids in *how to think* while not making many judgments and not holding too many convictions. But it's difficult to help students sharpen their thinking skills when you cannot really challenge them at all, and I couldn't challenge anyone because I didn't have strong convictions about anything. Or so I thought. It turned out that I had a few strong convictions that would get me into trouble later on.

But for now, since we are talking about process and about my confusion upon meeting some fundamentalist Christians on my first day on campus, we can just say that this was the beginning of figuring out that some processes—the ones that I cared about the most, the processes of teaching and serving my students well—weren't working as well as I wanted them to, because my process was built on some flawed ideas.

All teaching is ideological: any approach to teaching supports an underlying set of values while questioning or even denying others. I always would have nodded yes when reading that statement. Always. It's not like I didn't know that there are differences between teachers or that fundamental beliefs shape how one teaches.

But it is one thing to know there are differences, and to believe that they matter. And it's another thing entirely to believe that they matter *so much.*

At the time, my goal was to figure out how to teach you students well, despite the fact that we lived in different universes. There has always been a certain magic to me in the closing of my classroom door, when class starts and I get to learn about you. So to find that that magical time in the classroom was consistently punctuated with thoughts of *What is this kid thinking?* or *How are the two of us missing each other? What did he/she mean, and why doesn't my perspective make any sense to him/her?* led to some consternation and a desire to figure out a process that would make communication work between us.

There is also a certain magic to the closing of my office door, when a student comes to talk about their work or their grade or what they should major in. These are the few moments where I get to see deeper into your thinking, where I get a glimpse of your world, no matter how different you are from me. I've always sought to make those moments matter, and they have always been the moments that felt like they provided purpose and drove the magic of the classroom time.

But during that year, I noticed that my religious kids weren't happy. They would come to class, nod their heads, jump through the hoops to get a passing grade, and move on with a yawn. Everything I wanted for my classroom and for my students wasn't happening.

I remember sitting in my office with one young man, going over his paper, and pointing out that he needed more sources.

"Shouldn't a religious argument hold up in other contexts?" I asked. "Shouldn't you be able to point out ways that the principles of your argument are at work in the world if, in fact, your argument is a good one?"

"You want me to use sources for other viewpoints, but I don't share those other viewpoints," he argued.

"But can you point out why you don't share them or why you disagree with them?" I asked.

"Why?" he asked. "Those are all just propaganda."

I blinked. "Propaganda?"

"Yeah," he said. "Those writers are manipulating information to get readers to agree with them."

I blinked again. "Of course they are. That's why you're writing a paper, too. The sources that you agree with could be considered propaganda. The writer you cited would be considered propaganda to people that don't agree with him or his methods."

My student shook his head and turned away from me almost in disgust. "No, it isn't propaganda. I'm not manipulating reality. I'm pointing out a principle that is true. When people manipulate information to convince readers that lies are true, then *that* is propaganda. Why should I waste my time on that kind of 'research'?"

"But couldn't people see your sources as simply manipulating information as well? Couldn't your viewpoint be labelled propaganda?"

He was quiet. I thought I'd caught him or made him think. But no.

"They would just be wrong. They would just be mistaken."

What is with these kids that they think in such black and white terms? I wondered to myself. *How can I possibly navigate these conversations effectively? How do I connect with them?*

If I couldn't understand their perspective or connect with them in any fundamental way, then I couldn't teach them to think well, to communicate about their beliefs effectively, or to engage with others effectively.

One of my very strong, very narcissistic convictions was that I *needed* to be able to teach these kids well. Or they *needed* me to teach them. Or *both*.

* * *

It took several months to recover from my disbelief that my super-educated perspective was actually irrelevant to my religious kids. After several conversations like the one about propaganda, I decided I wanted to understand the world these students came from. How do I reach them? I wondered. There must be a way.

Well, I'm a rhetoric teacher. We are into Looking at the Other Perspective, Investigating The Arguments of the Opposing Viewpoint. Trying to figure out what their epistemology is, their methodology, the structure of their argument.

So I decided to study my Christian students.

I needed a student that would let me ask questions, and could articulate their fundamentalist perspective. And it needed to be a student that I liked, one that engaged my respect. I needed an admirable, articulate fundamentalist who didn't mind being asked a few questions by a feminist outsider.

It would take literal magic to produce such a student, I thought.

Strangely, I had several such students. This book is for them.

Usually, instructors write for other instructors. Or for tenure committees. Conversion narratives are often written for the writer's peers, and apologetics are, sadly, often written to other believers. This book is a little strange because it's written in retrospect, to students who played a part in the transformation of my worldview, but never knew it. As a result, it's a bit confessional: I want them to know that they mattered. It's also a bit instructive: I'm their teacher, after all, and in many cases I'm old enough to be their mother. It's also reticent in some ways that might seem odd to non-student readers. Since I'm writing to my students, I stick to the kinds of stories and comments I might tell in class or share in my office. Other parts of my story are for other audiences ... and other books.

It was hard to figure out exactly how to approach a book that is a letter to past students. I wanted to write about the vocation of teaching, my students, and about the confusion of encountering Jesus Christ as a postmodernist. But those are hard things to write about. If I talk about those subjects too much, it might make it difficult to, say, assign my own book in my future classes. (That's a joke. I wouldn't do that.)

Furthermore, over the years that I taught all of you, I was often confused about what I thought about these meta-topics, like the meaning of teaching, and how Christianity figured into teaching. How can I write about the cognitive confusion and dissonance that accompanied those years of discovering reality? I would have to come up with some bizarre metaphor for the way I believed several contradictory things at once.

So I decided to write a book about a manageable topic. Something you students could *really* use. Something that is very straightforward, and does not require ambitious—or amphibious—metaphors.

This book is about how to write a college paper.

CHAPTER TWO

LESSON 2: WRITE ABOUT SOMETHING YOU BELIEVE IN.

Today we are talking about invention, the process of discovering topics for research. There are a million ways to invent the topics for your papers, but they all begin with you. Strangely, the things that make you cry or want to hit somebody might also be a great place to start with searching for academic research projects. It sucks to have to sit and write ten pages about something you don't care about. So you need to choose things you have some investment in.

Investment means that you care and want to learn, that you have some stake in the knowledge that emerges from learning about the subject. Writing should have an element of discovery to it, and I want you to discover something with each major assignment. You can't make discoveries if you just write about things you think will make a good paper topic or things that you think sound smart or things that you think I want you to write about. What I want is for you to be willing to take a risk and own the things that affect you as your research topics in this class.

You have to balance the emotional stakes that you have in your work and in your research questions. In some way, anything you care about or are invested in will come back to your relationships and people you have cared about. So you need to think critically about how to balance the things you want to know with your feelings about the people you know. For example, when I sat down to write this story for you, I decided to only write about students that did two things: First of all, they engaged my affection. Second of all, they engaged my respect. I did this because I don't have nice things to say all the time. But if I am writing critically about people I liked and admired, then I can be more confident that even my critical comments are not made in a spirit of meanness. After all, despite everything that happened, I still loved these students in the end. We will probably never agree on everything, and no doubt I interpret Scripture differently than many of them did, but we have the same Savior.

It's hard to figure out how to write about the things you care about. But really, if writing a paper is going to be worth the time, you need to write about things that you believe matter.

* * *

While many writers love to keep journals, I have always found that keeping one is an exercise in wasted effort and frustration. This is due to the fact that one can never tell on a given day what will actually end up being of importance in that day. One can hardly predict which conversations will come up a week later or which interactions will have far-reaching influence. When one looks back over a few years, which daily habits will have led to errors in thinking, or which habits will have led one into new relationships or broken old relationships? One cannot tell at the time of the events. But when one looks back, patterns emerge and the patterns explain how we get to unexpected places.

On my first day teaching in the fall of 2014, I passed out the syllabus, did my first-day spiel, and had everyone introduce themselves. It was my fourth semester teaching at this particular campus now. After introductions, I asked students to take out a piece of paper and write an answer to this question: "What do you want to get out of this class?" I asked a few other questions about what makes a classroom comfortable and likes/dislikes about teachers. I did not require students to put their name on the paper. I did not ask the question about what book they had read recently.

That afternoon I sifted through the papers at home, and one stood out to me. In response to the question "What do you want to get out of this class?" there were two words written on the page: "Literate magic." Black ink, forceful up and down strokes. It was a boy's writing, and if it were a font, I would call it Jailbreak.

Or maybe I would call it Literate Magic. The phrase didn't make perfect grammatical sense, but the more I thought it, I liked it and its possible implied meanings. "What do you want to get out of this class?"

"Literate magic, please."

I hung the paper on the board above my desk. It fluttered there for the entire year. Off and on over the next two semesters, as I taught this student, I looked at that paper with varying degrees of affection, annoyance, malice, and grief.

A few weeks into the class, as I was walking around and checking on groups of students while they worked on a citation exercise, I noticed which student's handwriting matched that paper. He was one of the homeschoolers, who sat in the third row all the way over against the wall. His name was Grey, a seriously Southern boy's name.

I had already noticed this kid for a number of other reasons, so it didn't surprise me to discover that he was the literate magic one. He didn't actually look at people, he glared and then slid his eyes away. He was brilliant but lazy and thought he knew a lot, but he tended to write papers that were lists of claims with very little real discussion of ideas. He didn't engage with other perspectives well. He leaned against the wall a lot and always seemed sleepy. I would've laid money he played video games too much and wrote strange free-verse poetry with misplaced adverbs.

But I *liked* him. He wanted to talk to people, wanted to express himself well, but he just wasn't practiced at it. I could tell by the way he listened and watched what was happening around him that he was thinking about what was being said. There was something about the way he took in the classroom, the things I said, the way he frowned and fussed and got unsure of how to disagree that was just likable to me. I just liked him.

Also, he reminded me of my younger brother. I didn't know why he reminded me so strongly of my brother. He didn't look like my brother or talk like him, no mannerisms were the same. But there was some intangible similarity. I wondered many times why this student bothered me so much. But then I would push the thought away.

* * *

Christian students—especially you super-Christian ones—have favorite paper topics. The topic of marriage is a favorite, along with the virtues of home schooling, the evils of abortion, topics related to American history and Christian values, critiques of celebrity culture, and freedom of expression or issues related to the correct interpretation of the Constitution. Several of them are issues related to hermeneutics, something that you Christian students are practiced at discussing without even realizing that there is something called "hermeneutics." You don't realize how much Bible study has actually taught you about certain "academic" debates, but that's a different topic.

Grey, predictably, decided to write a major research paper on gay marriage.

The first draft was a list of facts and items related to gay culture, etc. And there was an argument made from the Bible. I suggested he diversify some source material and double check a few things, and asked that he please find a way to not use the Bible in an academic paper.

"But I am making an argument based on a biblical principle. Why wouldn't I use the Bible?" he argued.

"If you can't make the argument using something else, then you need a different topic for this class," I said. "Surely if you are making a sound argument, there is other evidence, other sources, and other arguments that can be made for your position."

He glowered a bit.

"Also, you need to acknowledge some kind of opposite argument in the paper. Show some understanding for people who hold a different view from you."

He looked directly at me. "I don't understand their view, though."

"Well, maybe you could spend some time reading some of their sources and try to see their viewpoint. Like, you could try to understand their view."

"I don't though."

"You haven't tried. You could try."

"Why would I do that?" he asked in an annoyed tone. "I'm not going to agree with them, so why would I read stuff that argues for their side?"

I sighed. "You know, it doesn't always have to be so adversarial. You do have things in common with people you disagree with, and finding those things can help you to argue for your own perspective more clearly . . . because you can connect your viewpoint and their viewpoint to some shared values."

He looked at me blankly. "Shared values?"

"Yes. Everyone wants the same thing."

"Like what? What shared values do I have with people who see the world in a totally different way than I do?"

"Like love. Everybody wants love."

"That's generic."

"No, it's not. Love is a fundamental need for people. You have one way of getting love. Other people are different from you, but still need love. That's something you have in common; it's simply a truth about human beings that connects them to each other. You should be able to acknowledge the basic things you have in common with other people."

He narrowed his eyes a little at me, then shrugged and turned away. "I'm not going to write about that," he said.

I bit my lip. Lecturing an eighteen-year-old guy on how to

include love as a universal value in a paper was probably not the best use of my time. The poor kid probably didn't really get what I was talking about anyway, or he hadn't had adequate life experience to see what I was getting at. Essentially, I was trying to encourage him to see other people as fellow human beings, people who were more similar to him than they were different. This tactic never did work with him, but I just couldn't give up.

"Well, you can pick something else. Family, maybe—everyone wants a family, people to come home to. Or something else you can think of. But find a value you have in common with these people and acknowledge it as a point of reference, as the reason that both sides make the arguments they do."

He looked annoyed. I had probably gone way over his head. "I don't mean to confuse you," I said as he made his way to the doorway, where he turned around and leaned against the doorframe.

"You're not confusing me," he said, but his eyes were still narrowed and his eyebrows furrowed as if he was thinking about something.

"Why do you think—" he stopped. "*Why* do you think people need love?"

Instantly my red-alert went off for a question that I didn't want to answer.

"Why?" I repeated, partly to clarify and partly to give myself a second to think.

"Yeah," he said, and repeated himself: "Why do *you* think people need love?"

"Well, we're all born needing certain things in order to function properly."

"Yeah, but—*why* do *you* think people need love? What do *you* think?"

"Well," I paused and looked around myself, like the answer might be written across my desk or something. "I'm not sure," I admitted. "I'll think about it."

Leaning against the doorway, he looked down at the floor then. I think he felt my discomfort and felt apologetic, although not enough to actually apologize.

"I'll email you a new draft this weekend," he said. Then, he left. I watched the space in the doorway where he had stood for a moment. Something hurt. He had seemed to really want me to answer the question.

It is not an infrequent occurrence for a student to ask me a question that is essentially asking about my worldview. I didn't have a stable worldview and it had never bothered me to give relativistic answers. In fact, that often seemed to be what students liked. But Grey never liked my answers. At the time, I thought that maybe Grey just wanted to hear an adult he liked agree with his worldview in some way, or maybe he just wanted to know something personal about me in order to connect with me or with the class more. Maybe he didn't have as secure a world at home as I had thought he did, and he was trying to connect with other parent figures. I couldn't shake the feeling that I had somehow failed him by not answering this one question, but when I looked at the empty Grey-shaped space in the doorway, I felt lost.

I don't know what to say to you, I thought. *I want to say something that is true and something that helps you, but I don't know what you need in the first place.*

* * *

The weekend is not long enough when students are sending you drafts. It takes forever to wade through their draft, think about it, make good comments, and then send it back. Only to receive it again five hours later, with two sentences changed.

But I digress, my dears.

I might have been close to forgetting that moment with Grey. I can do that: get busy, get working, and forget the moments when I wish I understood a student better. Even for a kid like Grey, who had somehow engaged my heart and had me open to whatever bizarre questions he might pose, I could still push it all away and forget.

Except that, of course, he emailed me. With a new draft. But also with a reminder: *Have you thought about my question? Why do you think people need love?*

I stared at the screen. He had asked me again. I mean, the kid had balls, I would give him that. But I didn't feel that I could—or should—answer this question. I made lengthy comments on his draft and sent it back.

He wrote back: *But you didn't answer my question.*

I stared at the screen for the second time in less than an hour.

I felt a little ticked off. He was badgering me. But also: I didn't like it that he could tell I was avoiding the question. I didn't want him to think that I didn't have an answer or wasn't sure what to say. I wanted him to accept my lack of response and forget about digging into what I personally thought about anything.

I'm not comfortable answering that question, I answered, and he didn't bring it back up.

After I sent it, my internal editor kept taunting me: *You worded it so that he would think you have an answer but don't want to share it. When in reality you don't know how to answer a very simple question.*

During the next few classes, I barely looked at him. There was a sense of chagrin and apology about him, like he wished he hadn't harped on the question at all. I think he knew that I was bothered by the question because I didn't have an answer to it.

A few years later, I would sit with a colleague in a different office on a different campus and tell this story, about how this student asked why people need love.

"Why would that question be such a big deal?" my colleague would ask with a laugh. "I mean, who cares what he thinks about people or why you think people are the way they are?"

I would laugh too, but I was just fake laughing. I can't believe that anyone would fail to understand the significance of that question.

The question assumes that all people are similar in certain ways, and how I answer that question reflects what I think a person is. Who are we, and why do we need the same thing? If I know why people need love, then I should also have a complimentary theory or answer to how to prevent the things that a lack of love produces: suicide, torture, terrorism, you name it. What does this question *not* relate to?

Sometimes I don't feel like I care about anyone, and sometimes I love people. Which feeling is "real," and which one addresses the needs of people around me? Does anyone I know really need me or need love from me? Are the connections between people something we make up, or are they biological impulses, or *both*?

If people don't need love, why do I care so much about my

students? Why care what a half-educated neo-goth gamer asks me? Why wish so badly that I could give him the gift of enjoying the people around him? Every time I tell myself that I don't need to care about what that student asks, because I'm better than that, I know I'm lying. I actually *do* care. I don't think I'm too good to care what these kids think. So why do I care? Are my feelings real? Do my students need me to care? Or anyone to care?

Many times I thought to myself, *I must be making all of this up. Surely it's not really that important.*

* * *

Grey might have eventually faded from my memory if not for one final thing.

After months of wrangling here and there over whether he could manage to use something other than the Bible as the basis for an argument, whether or not he could give credit to any opposing arguments, whether he could analyze a short story featuring a lesbian hero without making sardonic and rude comments, whether or not he could acknowledge the strengths of a pro-choice line of logic, whether or not he could manage to read *some* of the sources I offered him for some of his papers, and several months after he had asked me why people need love, he made a comment that not only bothered me by itself, but it made all of the previous conversations I had had with him haunting.

I don't even remember what we had begun talking about, but he had loitered after class to bring something up, and we were debating opposing sides (of course). At some point I decided to point out that he was arguing from the standpoint of his faith and not logic. Somehow in this bizarre conversation, his faith became the central point of the discussion, which was something I always tried to avoid. I didn't want Grey to feel like I was attacking his faith, and from my standpoint, I wasn't. I just wanted him to try to think about other perspectives.

"You have to be able to argue from the standpoint of logic, not just from your faith," I said.

"That doesn't mean anything," he said, somewhat disgustedly. "What would I use for logic or reason if I wasn't going to use my faith?"

"No, I didn't mean that I don't want you to use your faith," I said apologetically, though that was in fact what I had just said. "It's just that someone who is not a Christian can't understand you. Don't you want to be understood?"

"I don't know," he said. "I want to be understood but— but—" He paused.

"But only by Christians?" I asked pointedly.

"No—I mean, I was just confused about how to respond there for a minute, because I'm not sure that I'm actually saved, and I know I should work on that—"

Grey was probably planning on going somewhere with that statement. But I didn't let him.

"What do you mean?" I said.

"I mean, I'm not sure that I am actually saved, but I still want—"

"What do you mean, you're not sure? How do you keep trying to argue for this viewpoint when you are not sure of it?"

"I am one hundred percent convinced that Christianity is true. I am just not sure that I am saved." He was standing in the doorway of the classroom, wearing black cargo pants with his backpack over one shoulder. He put his hand up on the side of his head and looked down at the ground, and for a second I could read embarrassment in him. "I know I should work on that," he said again.

I said something that was an attempt to be soothing and gentle; I don't remember what. Something that was supposed to be encouraging, but I'm sure it was obvious that I didn't know what to say. The conversation became awkward and Grey looked down, flicked his bangs out of his eyes, said something about seeing me next class, and left.

I stood behind my empty lectern, looking at an empty room. Looking at the spot where Grey usually sat, kind of glowering, kind of curious about the people around him, smiling awkwardly when he had something smart to say.

I had felt my heart hurt for students several times, but this was different.

I felt pain at the way he looked down and away, like he was embarrassed to admit that he was unsure about his faith. I hurt for him, definitely. And there was something else: rage.

Who would tell Grey that he wasn't good enough? That insecure kid, who was so prickly and mean and curious about people around him? Who would tell him that he wasn't part of the club that he was arguing for? What effing jerks would do that?

I wanted to burn down his church. Or find his parents and gouge their eyeballs out with a spoon. How dare they tell him things that make it so that he would stand in the doorway and look down at the floor like that?

I'm going to find them and tear their limbs off. They have it coming. Telling Grey stuff that makes him hurt.

This was irrational, and I did not care.

I actually still don't.

The moment when he had stood in the doorway, put his hand up to his head and looked down: the Intangible Similarity to my brother had never been so loud.

It's the way he struggles with himself, I acknowledged in my heart with such a pang that I think I actually made a noise while standing there alone in my classroom. It's the embarrassment that he doesn't think he's getting something right, something fundamental to who he is. The Intangible Similarity was existential conflict and pain.

I know where that kind of conflict and pain leads boys.

There is a box of secret memories in my heart, and in one of them, I am standing over my brother's coffin, looking at his body, reduced to an object now that he is gone.

That is not said to be melodramatic. It is a real memory, and it is indicative of a very real consequence of the kind of internal conflict I can see in many of my students.

That memory floats under the surface whenever I am teaching. My students are about the age my brother was when he died. I see him in many of my students. I see him in many of the boys.

I rarely cry because of it, but I did tear up that day as I was standing in my classroom, looking at Grey's empty spaces, the space where he would sit during class, and the space where he had stood in the doorway.

I will not care so much, I told myself.

Yet when I sat down to write you all a story about meeting God, what did I write about? What do I always tell you? The things that make you feel are where you start to ask good research questions, where you have an investment that can lead you somewhere.

* * *

I kept my distance from Grey after that. But the damage was done. I mulled and mussed and wrestled with what to do. The year was almost over and I wouldn't ever see Grey again. While I couldn't imagine that there would ever be another student just like Grey, I was sure there would be other Christians that would catch my heart and upset me. There were so many Christians at that school. What was I going to do? I couldn't burn down all their churches. Only because I didn't want to go to jail, not because church burning wasn't something I wouldn't consider if I thought it might save my kids.

I have got to be able to explain to them when they're wrong, I said to myself. Something felt startled inside. I had said "wrong." Surely I didn't want to tell kids they were wrong, or to believe something different than what they'd been raised to believe. Telling people what to believe isn't my job. That was wrong.

So then what? I thought desperately.

No, I *do* want to be able to tell them when they're mistaken. I want to be able to tell them when their beliefs are helping them and when their beliefs are hurting them. Grey wasn't the one who had failed. I had failed, because I didn't have a knowledgeable way to encourage him out of that religious self-rejection. I wasn't able to offer a cogent opposing argument when it mattered.

I would mull this over while I fussed around my office, graded papers, made copies. Yes, I would say to myself as I marched around with my coffee mug, *when a boy stands in the doorway and says, "I don't know if I'm saved," I need to be able to talk to him about the concept of being "saved," and the concept of being "loved." I need to be able to save him from himself, for God's sake.*

But to do that, I realized I had to figure out what exactly they do believe. And what I believe. And how to talk to them about it.

I needed to do some research. Study them. Learn how they interpret the Bible.

Only then could I save them. From themselves.

FACTS ABOUT HYDRAS: THEY ARE REAL.

A three-headed hydra was strolling down the street, and she passed the window of a bookstore. All three of her heads immediately perked up and began looking at different books through the window.

It is a fact that, as mythic creatures, hydras are universally drawn to books. The irreducibility of great stories draws them in.

Checking her purse, the hydra noted that she had some extra money and could buy a new book. She decided to go inside the store and look around.

This turned out to be an unfortunate choice, as a great deal of bickering ensued between her three heads. One wanted a book about writing, one wanted a comic book, and one wanted something Greek, although it wouldn't make up its mind about which Greek book it felt like buying.

The hydra sighed.

"Maybe there is a book that all three of us will like?" she suggested hopefully to her other heads, but they got fussy and looked away.

Then the hydra noticed people staring whenever she

would talk to her other heads, and it made her feel slightly embarrassed.

"Please stop arguing in public," she requested of her other heads. "It makes people notice that we are *here.*"

"No one believes in us. Therefore, it's not a big deal if they see us," chided one head.

"That's not how it is at all," said another head. "It's more like, they don't tend to see us because they don't believe we are real."

The hydra thought for a few minutes. It was really tragic, the way that people just looked through her and didn't seem to believe that she existed. They really needed to be aware of the reality of hydras. The facticity of hydras, as opposed to the mythology. After all, people can't be expected to believe in something they don't *know* about!

"I know what we can do," said the hydra. She went to the part of the store that has little journals and fancy pens. She picked out a new blank journal and a pen, a green one. She preferred green pens, because they matched her skin, which meant she could tuck them behind her ear and they weren't so obvious. That way, she always had a pen handy, but it wasn't a glaring fashion faux pas when it didn't really match her outfit. When does a pen really match one's outfit anyway?

With her purchase complete, the hydra went home and sat down at the dining room table with her new book and pen.

Facts about Hydras, she wrote carefully on the front of the notebook. She opened to the first page, and wrote: *#1. I'm a hydra.* The hydra looked at #1. Then she wrote: *#2. I might be the only one.* She looked at #2.

"That cannot be true," pointed out one of the other heads.

"Are we sticking to the facts or not?" quipped the other head.

"Just because we haven't *seen* any others, doesn't mean there *aren't* any others," acknowledged the hydra. She contemplated #2 for one more second, and then she scratched it out with confidence. "Surely there are others," she said to her other heads. "After all, we must stick to the facts about hydras if we are to convince people that we are real."

She wrote a new #2. And then wrote: *I am real. Hydras are real.* She sat back, tucked her green pen behind her ear, and folded her arms. "Now that is real," she said to her other heads in a satisfied tone.

Then she went into the kitchen to make some afternoon tea.

CHAPTER THREE

LESSON #3: DO YOUR RESEARCH.

Part of why you should choose something you're invested in to write about is because your emotional or intellectual investment will naturally help you generate questions about the topic. To answer those questions, you need to do something we like to call "research." Some of you think of research as clicking around on the internet and reading whatever garbage comes up. Some of you think of it as finding one salient piece of information and acting like that's enough to build an argument on. Some of you act like research is something I'm supposed to do for you.

To research well, you really need to change your thinking about it in several ways. First, "research" is the practice of finding two things: information, and connections, or meaning. You need both of these things to emerge from your research. "Information" is the facts and info you didn't know about your topic, and "connections" or "meaning" is the significance of that information.

Second, you need to think of research as any sort of

information gathering. Why can't talking to people who know more than you, be research? Or visiting somewhere to see something for yourself? Reading is a great way to research, but it's not the only way. In fact, I have found that discovering connections is actually done better by talking to knowledgeable people, experts in whatever I'm researching.

The third thing is this: authority of your sources is ridiculously important. You can spend hours reading about your topic, and if what you read wasn't written by smart people who really know the topic, then you're not in possession of any better information at the end of your reading time. You can talk to people, but if they're extremely narrow minded about the connections that are important in their area of expertise, or if they're just not insightful people, then you're not necessarily gathering helpful research.

If you want to learn about something, you need to carefully select a few sources of information that get to the heart of the topic and teach you the internal workings of that particular subject.

That's why, when I decided to study Christianity, I decided to study the Bible. It's the shortest, surest way to figure out what the hell is wrong with Christians.

* * *

"I want to study Christianity," I explained to my advisor, Kenneth. His eyebrows went up, then down. "What about it?"

"How did Christianity, as a belief system, become so powerful in the Roman empire? I mean, what exactly made it so *attractive* to people? I want to study the non-biblical literary record of their arguments."

I handed Kenneth a short proposal I'd written and a list of the texts I wanted to explore. I already had a good foundation in Roman rhetorical texts and history, so the list was aimed at integrating Christian and pagan polemics.

"This is a long list," Kenneth said.

"Well, I have to start broad, since I'm really starting at the beginning as far as my knowledge base is concerned," I conceded. "I need a year to produce really good work in this area, probably. But if you'll direct it, then I can get credit for it, and I'll have the time I need to study and figure out some potential answers to my questions."

Kenneth pushed the paper aside, leaned back in his chair, and put his arms behind his head, the way he did when he was thinking.

"What is the real question here?" he asked.

This is one of the reasons I love Kenneth; it's also why I picked him as my advisor when I had arrived in the doctoral program. He knows that "intellectual pursuits" are only ostensibly intellectual: really, there is something personal at stake, some internal debate that drives the will to spend the hours upon hours studying something. He's willing to ask questions about what I really want and what I really think. From the first time I met him (my first day on the campus), he and I were an ideal match. We had a similarly cynical view of university administration, a similar method of finding our identity in teaching and shepherding our students, and a similar penchant for sitting around and talking in circles about philosophical and worldview issues. Within a few weeks of meeting each other, we had easily fallen into a parental relationship where I asked his opinion on almost everything and he helped to guide my writing career, ensuring that I knew which editors and writers to engage with. In my third year in the program, Kenneth and I would write a textbook together and design new writing classes for the university. He was well known in our field, and my association with him would constantly pay off for me.

I dreamed of being him. This relationship was far too important to me personally and professionally, and the loss of it later would both wound me deeply and free me.

"The real question—" I repeated and trailed off, as I thought about how to articulate my answer.

"Yes," said Kenneth emphatically. "What are you really trying to learn?"

"How to respond to some of my students," I said. I had already told him a bit about Grey, but I offered a more detailed version of my interactions with him, complete with my internal conflicts and questions.

"I would kill myself if I had to teach out there where you work," said Kenneth distastefully and shook his head.

"No, you wouldn't," I said confidently. "You would hang in there and try to figure out what to say to them, just like I am."

"I don't know," he said, shaking his head. Kenneth had always been in large urban environments, and he was in his sixties. It was hard for him to imagine my classroom world. Of course, a few years earlier, I wouldn't have been able to imagine it either.

"If I understand the origins of their faith, then I can understand it in its contemporary form better," I pointed out. "It would be interesting to see if the rhetorical practices of earlier Christians align with my students' practices."

Kenneth nodded, pursed his lips, and thought for a minute. "You're okay doing this study with an atheist?"

I laughed. "You think I would rather find some indoctrinated director who won't ask me hard questions?"

Kenneth ran his fingers through his bushy hair. "I can find you someone, if you want. Jackie comes from this . . . particular background," he said, waving his hand over my proposal. "I mean, I think her dad was an elder in a church and everything."

I leaned back and put my hands on my head just like he often did. "No. I want you to direct it. Ask me hard questions. Make me figure it out."

"Okay, we can do that," he said. He picked up his pen and signed off on the proposal, then sat looking at his signature on the page for a minute.

"There's one problem with these things," he said after a minute. There was a new tone in his voice. He looked at me and said with some hesitation, "Sometimes researchers go native. I think it's a hard temptation to resist. It's hard to keep one's objectivity when trying hard to understand how another group thinks."

I nodded, listening. "Has that happened before . . . with one of your advisees?"

He shrugged. "It did once. It was okay, he finished the program just fine. But . . . he developed a different agenda while he was here. After all," Kenneth said thoughtfully, "he thought he had discovered the *truth*." He looked at me. "Just don't go native on me."

"I won't," I promised.

* * *

I had no idea what I was getting into. For the next year,

everything related to the Roman Empire and the rise of Christianity was fair game for this study I undertook, and while I spent a year doing this, I barely made a nick in the amount of information that it is possible to ingest on these topics. I ended up concentrating on the earliest apologetic treatises for Christianity, following these through the time of Augustine.

There are many texts written about early Christianity, and there are researchers who have undertaken to write about their academic encounters with historical Christianity. Some of them have done an awesome job. That is not my task here, for several reasons. A discussion of early Christian texts isn't what I want to talk about with my students, and this book is for them. It is sufficient to say that I spent a year wading through early Christian thought and writers, and I even traveled to interview folks who were better read than I was. And holy eff, was it overwhelming.

During that year, I often reported to my students on what I was reading and shared interesting things I had found, and I shared parts of an article I had written with them. To my surprise, my Christian students loved to hear about the pagan objections to Christianity from the ancient world. Hearing that they had been characterized as ignorant or culturally deviant, they would laugh. "It's the same as today!" they would say. "Yes, it is," I would agree, enjoying the moments when their guard came down and they felt they could laugh about themselves and the mischaracterization of their beliefs that was, I have to say, strangely consistent throughout history. I seem to remember one class where I explained that some early Christian community had done a poor job of explaining what communion was and, as a result, the surrounding community thought that Christians practiced human sacrifice and drank blood. I believe that a hilarious theoretical discussion connecting vampirism and Christians ensued.

But that is probably just a trick of my memory, since such a discussion is clearly not suited to a college writing class, and I would never have allowed discussion to get off track in such an obscene fashion.

* * *

There are some real dangers for any skeptic who decides to have an in-the-dirt encounter with Christianity. You have to really deal with the Bible, for one. This is like committing to an Old Testament-style night battle. You may not lose outright, because you can always refuse to surrender. But you won't win.

The more that I read the Bible, the more that the question of whether or not this faith was real became a pressing, daily reality for me. It was like there was always someone knocking on the door, and I was trying to work and study without noticing the incessant knocking. The biblical record was impressive, and the historical veracity of this faith was odd: It was like Jesus Christ had arrived in history, *despite* history, instead of Christianity emerging in response to a historical exigence. I was starting to see how a faith-based epistemology contradicted the epistemological values that I generally espoused. The mental pressure and emotional pressure was rough, and I paid a serious price in all of my relationships, because I was always withdrawn and frustrated.

Kenneth's request that I not "go native" was always playing in my mind. But in some ways I was not only starting to feel protective of my Christian kids, I was also starting to identify with them . . . and even *envy* them. Then I would have a day where I would reject it all and get back to business, back to my empirical mindset. Then I would read a letter of Paul's and spend days studying it, admiring it, enjoying it. Then the whole mental and emotional cycle would start over.

I was tired. I thought I was tired of studying. But really I was running in circles trying to protect myself from having to make difficult decisions. Trying to protect one's self has a cost: it halts emotional response to goodness and the ability to accept love and grace. In my darker moments, I would consider quitting teaching. *To do what?* I would ask myself. Teaching was my identity, and I had set myself this goal of "understanding" my fundamentalist students, so in order to maintain my identity as "a good teacher," I needed to achieve that goal. Perversely, God used my lame-ass attempts at a self-generated identity to keep me moving toward himself.

During that year, I attended a conference with a few of my colleagues, and one of the breakout sessions featured a speaker who had completed a writing studies project looking at the rhetorical practices of fundamentalist students. In reading the description of her work, I was under the impression that this woman was much like me: she had had some fundamentalist kids in her class, had noticed some interesting coping strategies they used in their college work, and had set out to do a case study to describe these particular strategies and how they played out in a writing class. I was looking forward to hearing her speak and was hopeful that I might be able to connect with her personally.

As she shared with the small audience about how she came to the project and what her methods had been, I took careful notes. Then she got to where she made several conclusions about her fundamentalist study subjects.

Her conclusion was that her students' faith represented a crisis in literacy skills, that their faith-centric literacy had rendered them unable to engage with the work of a pluralistic classroom in a university setting.

This wasn't offensive to me because I thought she should conclude that these students had "The One True Faith" or something. It was offensive to me because it exploited young people and made them an object of derision among instructors, an older and more powerful group. Her assumption was that a literacy that was different from the norm was deviant, just because it was different, just because the students didn't engage with classroom norms in a way that demonstrated a literacy like her own. Furthermore, to say that students aren't "literate" when they are obviously practicing a different literacy seemed an abrogation of the role of the researcher. Aren't unique literacies interesting? There's a million niche literacies that are studied by university folks that are just that: niche literacies. Why should these kids be demonized for being another niche?

They have a question/answer session at these things. I sat there in my seat, steaming and wondering if I should ask a really pointed question. I could not come up with a way to ask about her biases that didn't sound antagonistic. I scrawled out a version or two of a question and showed them to my colleague, Karen. She shook her head at both of them and used her hands to make a "calm down" motion. I could not get myself into a mental frame that was peaceful though, so I stayed in my seat and did not ask any questions. I kept flipping through my mental file of my fundamentalist students who had done all of the "illiterate" things this researcher had identified. How dare she refer to my kids as illiterate! With every kid I thought of, I got angrier until I was sitting slouched in my seat with my arms crossed. I probably had my lower lip stuck out like a pissed-off brat.

The thing was, I didn't have a really good foundation from which to argue with her. I had all the knowledge required to question her and point out problems in her conclusions, but I had not yet organized my knowledge into a coherent understanding of what makes Christians different. I couldn't articulate exactly *why* she was wrong.

Later that evening, at dinner with Karen and our colleague Roger, I tried to express my frustration.

"When you care about your students, and then someone describes them as illiterate . . . I mean, I took that really *personally*," I explained to them, half in explanation and half in apology that I was *still* talking about it. Roger was chewing on a bite of a questionably cooked burger and seemed to be looking through me a lot. "Am I making sense?" I asked them. "Or do I sound like someone who just needs to take a break from teaching? Is this bothering me too much?"

Karen looked thoughtful. "I guess the question is what it means for your classroom. I mean, do you think it's a good idea to keep letting kids cite the Bible all the time or make faith-based arguments when in fact they have to go out into a world where they need to make other arguments?"

"I don't let them stick to faith-based arguments," I protested. "I just don't think that a faith-based argument should be characterized as illiterate."

"But you don't let them do it," said Karen. "It *is* considered illiterate, in some environments. You know that. That's why you won't let them do it. In that sense then, caring about them means explaining when it is illiterate to do certain things."

"So they need some rhetorical awareness. That doesn't make them illiterate."

Roger decided to finally swallow his bite and say something. "You know, I used to not care about the war that much."

I looked at him, wondering if something about teaching fundamentalist kids was going to be compared to being at war, a comparison that I was pretty sure I was going to find distasteful.

"A few years ago I had this young vet in my class, named Carson. He had served over there in Afghanistan, kicking in doors and stuff. And he came home and came to school at our campus. I really liked him," Roger paused, and I knew that he had probably never said out loud how much he had cared about this particular student. "After I had gotten to know him, one day he told a story in class about being shot at. He was so matter of fact about it, about how close he had come to being killed. I was sitting there at the front of the class listening to his story and how he told it, and I was suddenly so angry at whoever had shot at *him*. I was like, suddenly *upset* that anyone would shoot at him. It was like for a second I thought he was *mine*, and I was like, 'You are shooting at *my* Carson!'"

"But he's *not* yours," interjected Karen, obviously not loving the way this conversation was going. I couldn't blame her. Roger and I sounded like we needed therapy.

"He's not mine," agreed Roger. "And a second later I remembered that and calmed myself down. But I also couldn't really take back how that had felt for a minute—since then, I *feel* a lot more about the war. I hate it. I hate that there's people shooting at young people. At other Carsons."

Karen looked perplexed.

Roger put his burger down and looked at Karen pointedly. "Is it so wrong to think that one of them is like, *my kid,* the kind of kid I would want if I had one?" Roger asked rhetorically, waving his hand a bit and rolling his eyes at Karen. Roger was gay and married to his partner, so biological children were not in his future at the moment. I could see that this student had tapped into his wishes to be a father.

"It's paternalistic and infantilizing," Karen said grouchily.

"You're *wrong.* That's not what it is," Roger said emphatically and went back to his burger.

Karen made a rude sound of disbelief.

"We're fucking *humans*, Karen. We're not teacher robots or something," said Roger rudely. "Of course we care about them. They write us pages and pages about themselves."

The rest of dinner was quiet, and then we all separated in the hotel lobby to go to our rooms. The next day, the last day of the conference, I walked up to Roger in a different breakout session. "I like working with you," I said simply, giving him a hug. "I like you, too," he said and hugged me back. "It's okay to *like* the kids," he said reassuringly. Then he whispered in my ear, "It's okay if they're our *babies*," which made me laugh.

This seems like it can't be true, my dears, but it is: while you were writing papers railing against homosexuality, it was gay Roger that encouraged me to love you and to keep making you my object of "research."

* * *

This is also going to sound like I made it up, but I didn't: one of my previous students is the manager of a bar in town. These are the kinds of funny coincidences that happen when you teach in a small town for a few years. When I go downtown to the campus where I am doing my dissertation research, my friends and colleagues can't believe it. I know they're imagining some kind of truck stop dive, too.

But it's actually a nice bar. The kind that I can go to with my girlfriends, and the server will bring Mai Tais on a little green tray. Or Moscow Mules, if it's been a rough week.

The first time I met some girlfriends there, I was happily accepting my Mai Tai from a pretty brunette with a green tray, and I heard someone say, "It's my teacher!"

I turned around, and there was Jordan, looking all spiff in a black button down and slacks. Jordan is close to my age. Originally from California, he had joined the Army right out of high school and tried college classes after serving a few tours. He had worked part time at the bar then, and my writing class was actually the very first college course he ever took. After a few semesters he decided college wasn't for him, and he settled down to manage the bar and be a regular townie.

The thing is, when he was in my class, he often wrote about the crazy people that came in to the bar. So these days, when I drop by to chat with him, I ask him, "If you were taking my class now, would you be writing about me?"

"Definitely," he will say, grinning. "You would have no secrets. I would write about everything you said and did."

Honesty is usually a nice virtue. But not always.

Jordan, of course, had become a Christian. A little different from the other townies though, he had converted while in the Army. Even though he hadn't loved college classes, I discovered that he was actually very studious about his personal interests. When it came to Christianity, he was better read than most Christians. He understood Christianity's historicity, understood competing theological interpretations, and he knew the Bible well.

Once he discovered my new research commitments, the game was on. He was always ready to hear what I was up to and ask me good questions. He was a balanced source of information on how to interpret the Bible, and he knew how to get at my underlying anxieties. We had a great camaraderie which allowed for honesty, and I began dropping by weekly to enjoy a chat with him.

"So did you finish Romans?" he asked me at one point, when he had been pestering me to finish Romans and an accompanying set of notes he had given me from some study he had done on it.

"I finished it," I said in a dejected tone. "But nothing in it really contributes to what I'm working on right now, which is my meeting with Kenneth tomorrow. He's going to ask what I'm learning about, and I'm not sure what to say."

"Just describe the stuff you've been reading." Jordan was always really practical, which was helpful.

"I will," I said. "But I need to come up with some other connections between the texts and ways to explain a few answers to my research questions. I don't really have enough yet."

Jordan grumbled something.

"What?" I asked.

"Why does it matter if Kenneth thinks you have enough information or not? Isn't it just important for you to figure out some answers for yourself?"

"Well, in an ideal world, yes. But in the real world, I'm working on my doctorate and I'm supposed to be discovering some real information. And Kenneth is supposed to be helping me, so if I'm doing poorly, it reflects badly on him."

Jordan made a face. "Reflects badly on him? It sounds like the way he conceives of being a teacher is just . . . constricted."

I made a face. "What are you talking about?"

Jordan thought about it for a minute. "How would he explain his friendship with you? Why would he say he is friends with you, or why would he say he goes out of his way to do things for you?"

"He likes me? He cares about me?"

Jordan shook his head. "Would he say that he cares about you? What would he say?"

"He would say that I'm talented. That we get along well and have a good rapport."

"So he would take the 'care' out of it?"

I nodded. Jordan shook his drink a little to make the ice shift. "Why wouldn't he say he cares about you, like you would say about other students?"

"That's not how he conceives of student relationships."

Jordan looked disturbed. "Remind me not to send any of my kids to that university."

"You don't have kids."

"When I have them. Keep them away from you people."

"What, like you want to send them to some cloistered Christian school?"

"Probably not. Just don't want them around people who only conceive of the way they 'care' for people in sanitized ways like 'she's talented.'"

"I know that's not all he thinks. He would go out of his way for me."

"Would he? Why? Why would a materialist go out of their way?"

I laughed. "You're being dramatic. He's just like other people. He goes out of his way because it's habitual or he likes someone or he thinks it's his job or because it benefits him."

"Helping people is neither, though. In some way it costs us to help others, even if it also benefits us. And helping people is not habitual."

"It is for me. I help students out of habit."

"You help students because it's a major part of your identity. It's still self-centered."

Ah, that virtue of honesty.

"Isn't it a greater benefit to society to teach kids than it is a self-centered act on my part?" I asked. Jordan laughed.

"Society is fine without you, Kori. You don't do it to serve society. You would do it even if you didn't see a clear benefit to society."

"True," I said. "I would still teach. But as far as trying to teach well, that's a different thing. We do that for the love, Jordan."

"Who is 'we'?"

"Well, me. And anyone else who cares about students. Kenneth, too."

"Ah," Jordan tipped his head back. "Don't worry, I won't tell Darwin that you all are actually motivated by love."

"I didn't say that," I pointed out.

"You did, though. You say it in some way, in every conversation and in all your stories."

I played with my Mai Tai, turning the glass slowly on the tabletop.

"Jordan, why do people need love?"

Jordan didn't look surprised at this question, he just gave a slow nod while he processed it. Part of why I like him is that he can accept shifts in the conversation easily.

"That's just another way of saying that they need God. God is love. But people need love or God because they're sinners. They can't ever be good without help. So we need the help that is God, that is love."

"So . . . people need love because they're sinners. And love is God."

"Yeah. In a nutshell."

Well, there I had it. When Grey had asked me why people need love, I should have said, "Because they're sinners, Grey." Except no way was I going to say that to some kid who needed encouragement. Holy eff.

I explained this conundrum to Jordan. He had heard the story about Grey, and he knew where I was coming from.

"The thing is, though," he said slowly, "you're saying that you want to be able to tell students something that is true. And telling them that they are *fine* is not *true*."

"Well, I'm not going to say that we're all sinners. And that they're sinners. Come on, Jordan. I'm not some kind of preacher."

"You're a teacher. It's just a different kind of preacher."

I glared at him. "It is not. Being a teacher means helping students find their own ideas, not preaching at them."

"That's semantics. You know what I mean, anyway. Both teachers and preachers are guides of some kind."

"But I don't try to get them to agree with me. That's not the point. And I can't talk to them like that anyway, because we don't even agree on what's real or not, what's right or wrong, or what constitutes 'truth.'"

"Except for the love part. You and your students agree that people need love."

"One student. We were saying that people need love, and he asked me why," I parried, trying to correct Jordan.

Jordan shook his head. "You aren't doing all this work because of one kid."

"Well, no. I don't even know that kid anymore. But it kind of—" I waved my hand in an aggravated way. "It represents something. Other students. A way of understanding them."

"Your students aren't all the same person, though. There's not one way of understanding them. They're each different."

"They're each different, but they have some things in common. You can definitely understand a group better by understanding the things they have in common."

Jordan shrugged. "Well, one thing they have in common is a weird teacher."

Ah, the honesty.

Something struck me. "Jordan, when you were in my class, would you have even cared if I had wanted to understand your faith?"

He looked at me warily. "I'm not as worried about what people around me think as you are, Kori. I probably would have found the conversation interesting, but I wouldn't have been very heavily invested in it." He leaned toward me. "Besides," he said in a quieter tone, "I would have known that it wasn't really about me, anyway. You aren't trying to learn about your kids as much as you want to learn about you."

I probably flushed a little bit. "You sound like Kenneth."

That didn't even phase Jordan. "I'm pretty sure that *that guy* and I are not saying the same thing," he said.

I knew that while Kenneth and Jordan used similar words, they had completely different intentions and a different basis of meaning for their words. Jordan was always patient and would change the conversation if I didn't like it. A year or so later, he would admit to me that he could tell I didn't like the way that Christianity seemed to make sense of so many of my experiences, while at the same time, the story of a man who was God seemed incomprehensible to me. I felt like I was falling into a bad dream, where I wasn't sure what might be real and what wasn't. Nagging doubts would intrude in my conversations with Kenneth, and nagging doubts would intrude in my conversations with Jordan. Alone, by myself, I tried to do the postmodern squeeze and assure myself that an eclectic worldview was possible, doable, and even *better*. Internal consistency be damned.

But I was suffering from a constant internal argument between enumerating perspectives, and it exhausted me and slowly drained the research of creativity or enjoyment. What's more, that kind of existential confusion is hard to share with anyone else, and I felt increasingly lonely and isolated. "There's no such thing as a postmodern Christian" was a constant chorus from one side, and "There's no such thing as a unified, single truth" was the chorus from the other side.

I had achieved a certain academic mastery over the question of why Christian students didn't love my writing class, why they pushed back against university ideals of knowledge-creation, and why they seemed to be hung up on certain exclusionary university practices, like instructor issues with citing the Bible.

But my own confused worldview precluded me from having language for your perspectives in any phenomenological sense. Where did Christian ideas *come from*? Jordan would tell me I was arguing in a circle, and I knew that I did in fact circle back to the same questions, but how I had done that and what I had missed kept escaping me. I could explain the problem intellectually but I couldn't really get to where the problem came from. What was worse, I could see that there was a lacuna in my ability to describe the problem—but seeing that I was suffering a shortcoming in my ability to describe, solve, and explain a problem is different from seeing how to close the gaps in my understanding.

The gaps were just there. I cared that they were there, but I didn't know what to do about them.

This is what is commonly called an "intellectual crisis": when a person knows they need to figure something out and they are even driven to figure it out, and they can't do it using any of the intellectual tools available to them. It's frustrating and demoralizing. Teaching seemed less fun during this time, although quitting seemed like giving up, like letting somebody else beat me at a game that I should be able to win.

In my darker moments, I would decide that none of this should matter so much. Kids that aren't mine shouldn't matter so much. And if God wanted these intellectual problems solved, he should have helped out a little more, a long time ago.

There is a belief in Christianity that while God redeems us from sin, we still suffer consequences from it, both from individual sin and from the corporate/community sin of unbelief. The university culture that I had invested my time and effort in was a culture of unbelief. And I *had* embraced it, along with feminist theory and materialism. The consequence of this is the development of a mind that has trouble with reason, with reality, and with spiritual presence. It is a long and uncomfortable process to develop a new mind and shed an old one. For some time, both ways of thinking are in play. This creates a phenomenally uncomfortable inner dialogue that sometimes makes zero rational sense.

At several points over the years, I could have given up and retreated into a patchwork, vague version of Christianity. God would still have loved me, I would still have been a Christian, and life would have gone on.

Usually, when I wanted to retreat, I would recall classroom moments with students I couldn't quite reach, couldn't quite understand, and couldn't quite help. I really wanted to be able to talk rationally about your beliefs and mine, make sense for you of the disjunction between the university and the world, and ameliorate the stress of growing up by giving you some tools that would help you cope with all the unreasonableness out there. That's what teachers are supposed to do. It's what my teachers had always done for me, in the absence of strong parents, and it's what I wanted to do for you.

Then one day, the stress was really too much. I decided to tell my memory of all of my students, of Grey and the Intangible Similarity, to eff off. I was sitting in my office down town, and I was done. I was tired, I was depressed, I was done with Christianity. *Done*, people. I opened my office door with fresh resolve and the weight of Figuring Out Christians lifted from my shoulders. Who cared what *anyone* believed? I was done with this shit. Coexist and be gone, ye demons of worldview confusion.

It was the day of our university's homecoming parade, and I went down the hall to watch the parade with my friends and colleagues, a fresh *I'm-over-Christianity* spring in my step.

FACTS ABOUT HYDRAS: THEY ARE SKILLED AT LOOKING ON THE BRIGHT SIDE OF THINGS.

One day, the hydra stopped by the library. The research librarian was a very solid-looking Indian man with a thick patch of hair that looked as if it had been set on his head by an outside source. The hydra tried not to study his hair too closely as she asked him a few questions.

"Do you have any books about three-headed hydras?" she asked innocently.

The librarian looked at her quizzically. "Well, we have books about hydras. But usually they have more than three heads."

The hydra gasped. "More than three?!"

The librarian took a step back. He couldn't understand why the idea of more heads should be so disturbing to anyone. "Well, yes. In some of the stories, the hydra has fifty heads."

"GOOD GOD! THAT WOULD KILL ME!" hollered the hydra.

The librarian was visibly startled by all the yelling. He quickly regained his composure but was now obviously displeased with the hydra.

"Quiet, please!" he said. "There are students studying here, and two of the doctoral students are taking a break in the lounge!"

"So sorry," whispered the hydra as she glanced around the librarian and did, in fact, see two doctoral students peering at her from the lounge doorway, a half-done puzzle on the table behind them. She gave a rueful wave in their direction and turned back to the librarian.

"Well, where are the hydra books located?" she asked the librarian demurely.

"In with all the other material on mythology, on the fifth floor," grumbled the librarian.

The hydra searched all afternoon, but did not in fact find anything that could address her particular three-headed situation, why she was the way she was, or whether there were any other hydras currently at the university.

She did however, discover that traditionally hydras have emerged from Lake Lerna, one of the entrances to the Underworld.

The division of the self into competing narratives about reality is a gift to our race from Hades himself, the hydra wrote on her list of Facts about Hydras. She thought for a moment and then added, *Without the division of the self into competing narratives, one cannot actually make a choice between the disparate narratives.*

Feeling very satisfied that she had managed to look on the bright side even while learning that she was from Hell, the hydra went home and had some tuna for dinner.

CHAPTER FOUR

LESSON #4: ONCE COMPLETED, YOUR RESEARCH GUIDES YOUR ARGUMENT, NOT THE OTHER WAY AROUND.

We start papers by asking ourselves what we might want to argue about, but once the research is complete (or at a stage where we are going to call it complete for that assignment), we must try to ask a new question: What is the research showing me? Your research tells you what your claims and argument will be. Arguing for something effectively means arguing for the claims that your research revealed to you. You can't make information conform to your argument. Your argument needs to reformulate itself to take the research into account.

You don't have to prove something to me beyond a shadow of a doubt, but your claims should be supportable. If you keep arguing for something that isn't supportable, that's not because it's a good argument, it's because you're attached to that argument for some other, personal reason.

* * *

Homecoming of 2016 was the first time I had watched the parade from the coveted viewpoint of the English department lounge, on the twenty fifth floor. From that height, no one is recognizable, but the small brightly colored figures of the students marching made a snake of color down the middle of the road, by the trolley lanes, and curved around the green square of the park and the red roof of the coffee pavilion.

Jenny, my colleague who shared my love of all things sci-fi, was watering the plants. Roger was waving his hands about and noting that several of the plants had seen better days, and Kenneth was presiding over all of us with a merry and contented air, like a proud department dad. There was a French press on the table, the teapot was hot, and the smell of hot sugar permeated the air. The hum of the fridge and Karen's little Buddhist water fountain dribbling in the background completed the companionable tableau. The younger graduate students were wafting around in their earth mother skirts and Birkenstocks, and Matthew, the director of lower division studies, was laughing at something Sarah had just said. The top of Jenny's plastic watering container was screwed on crooked, and the water dribbled on the floor. I got up and walked over to her to fix it. I remember the feel of the plastic in my hand, Jenny smiling out the window while I fixed the lid. I handed it back to her and leaned toward the window, noting bright dots of students milling around on the pavement and that the parade was almost past the building.

Something fell past the window, causing a momentary shadow across my face.

"What was that?" asked Jenny, still smiling down toward the parade.

A few people blinked, turned, shrugged, and just barely paused in their conversations. The smell of hot sugar and fruit continued, Buddha dribbling in the corner.

Jenny turned toward Matthew, responding to something he had just said.

I pressed my forehead against the window, looking straight down the building, as close to the building as I could get from this vantage point to see—what I knew I would see. Dots were scattering quickly, the student crowd on the pavement changing shape quickly as it rippled away from the body that had just landed on the pavement. Luckily he didn't kill anyone else. He had jumped from the twenty sixth floor, from the window directly above us.

Time stopped.

What was he *thinking* in the last minutes up there, while a bunch of instructors took care of plants and laughed at jokes? Did I pass that young man on the elevator, on the stairs, or in the hallways earlier that day? Did he meet with anyone before that, have an appointment, discuss a paper or a grade? What had he written about? Had he sat in an office with an instructor and asked a question, and could the instructor have answered it in a way that would have made a difference? Was there an opportunity for a new connection, a life-saving connection or thought?

"I didn't even know him," I would hear several times over the next week. Would it have mattered if we did? I looked around the lounge at all of us, knowing I was the only one who realized what had just happened. Kenneth was toasting someone with his coffee. Matthew was laughing about something.

Roger caught my eye and winked in reference to some comment I was supposed to have just heard, but I hadn't.

Would it have mattered for that boy if he had known any of us? Did any of us have something to offer a heartbroken student, a hopeless student?

Here was a new question, and it hurt: Would it have mattered if the boy had known me? Not in the sense that I could necessarily stopped a young man from killing himself. But would I have had a meaningful alternative perspective to offer? Was there any *potential* that knowing me could have mattered for a student in distress?

Before long I left the building for the day. The wall of glass front doors was partially blocked by police tape. Everyone had to leave through the door furthest left so they didn't walk out into the debris of his body.

I didn't care if was morbid; I looked toward where his body was on the pavement. They had covered him, but the splashes of dark blood were visible.

Sick at heart, I walked the long way around the block to the big park that faced our building. Sitting on a bench, I looked up. I could see the broken window on the twenty sixth floor. That kid was determined.

Alone, I sorted back through the memories. Many students kill themselves every year, but I have specific faces to recall. I sort back through a boy who shot himself, two boys who hanged themselves, a friend from high school who hanged himself, and my younger brother, dead from intentional carbon monoxide poisoning at age seventeen.

Standing over his casket, the gray-face-that-wasn't-him-anymore posed the question: Does it matter what we believe?

Suicide tells me that ideas have consequences. They lead

somewhere. Does it matter what teachers believe? Do our ideas have consequences that we fail to take into account? How do we affect our students? How do we fail to affect our students?

I assume that teachers' worldviews matter, because I've been most influenced by teachers in my life. I adopted all my teachers' worldviews for myself.

When I walked down the hall to watch the parade that day, I had decided that I would just be comfortable in my ignorance, that I simply didn't have good answers but that I would retreat into self-talk about how "nobody can really know what's true" or "it doesn't really matter what I believe, I just need to teach them the material" or "if I can't understand it, no one really can, anyway."

But young people who commit suicide have always presented a challenge to me: Does it matter to me that their beliefs had real consequences? Do I have any intention of being better prepared for the next young man who wants to jump? And of course, these two questions harp on deeper issues of identity: What are people? What is a young man? Who am I? Why do I teach? What kind of relational transaction is happening when I have a conversation with someone fifteen years younger than myself? Who do I think they are? Do I think they are worth the difficulty of solving my own questions about human identity? What is a human being, and if they need love, what does that mean for a teacher?

These questions seem like things that teachers should never discuss with their students—at least not writing teachers. At least not me. I probably would never start a discussion with one of those questions, for a number of reasons. The students I teach are a bit young to be assaulted with heavy philosophical drama from their writing teacher, and they usually don't need the pressure of that kind of heavy-hitting discussion.

But my students ask all kinds of questions that I realize are tangentially related to these existential tensions and questions.

Examples of real questions that students have asked me: How do some people stay married for so long? Why has my best friend changed so much lately? Why do you think some people will die for something when others won't even get off the couch? Did you like my girlfriend? Are my boyfriend's pants ridiculously tight, or what? Should I just ditch college and go to Nashville to play music? Should I quit school and start my business? Do you think I should spend Christmas with my dad or my mom? Should I let my little brother come live with me? Should I spend so much time playing this video game? And over and over again: What do you think of this poem/story/genre-ically unidentifiable creative thing that I wrote? And their poems are about the feelings underneath the questions: Who am I? Why am I here? Will I be okay? Students will ask surprising things when they spend time around you, but the things they will write about can actually make you cry.

When students are in my office and talk about normal things or life things or what they are doing that weekend or whatever, I get a few small chances to respond to their thoughts. I cannot seem to offer responses that come out of some kind of consistent basis of understanding what the hell is going on around us. I am like a pilot who isn't actually sure how to fly the plane. And there's some mountains ahead. And we're supposed to survive this ordeal.

* * *

Is it any coincidence that on a day when I had decided to stop being concerned about my students, a young man jumps to his death in front of me? I remember looking up at the lovely blue sky like I was asking God. I didn't feel like I was being punished or something. I wasn't angry about the way the boy affected me. I knew then—as I know now—that God doesn't make people jump from buildings, just like He doesn't stop them, and I've had too much good fortune and near misses to think that Someone is trying to punish me or scare me.

So if I don't think it's intentional on "God's" part, then why do I wonder about "coincidences"? I mean, if God isn't intentional, then isn't everything a coincidence? What should I do with the tension between "God doesn't make people commit suicide" and the feeling that God is hunting me down, that there is no such thing as coincidence anymore, that every day has some extra dread as I wonder why He won't leave me alone? I again asked the sky, like it would answer. The sky seemed blank, unconcerned. Meanwhile, in the back of my mind, this other voice kept calling out answers to my questions, drawn from the biblical texts and the work of the apologists that I had been immersed in for so many months. I had a set of answers that dealt with my confused thoughts I had sitting there on the park bench, and they connected my history and my experiences and my feelings to what I was seeing in front of me, to what appeared to be reality. Perhaps it was because I was hurting, but the phenomenon of belief in the reality and consistency of Christianity was on me; there was actually a sound in my ears like an engine roaring or something, something bearing down on me. It was so loud that I had the urge to put my hands over my ears, like I could block it out. But I realized I didn't want to change. I didn't want to stay the same, and I didn't want to change.

A minute later I blocked it all out with some stern self-talk: *I'm just indoctrinating myself into this,* I remember saying. *I've spent too much damn time reading this stuff!* I reasoned that if I took a break, then maybe my conscience would settle down. Maybe I would go back to being comfortable with myself, find a way out of the internal bickering.

But, then again, didn't I always tell my students to let the research be an act of discovery, a way of growing up, of learning new ways to think? I sat on the bench and watched the police cars and the ambulance. My thoughts accused me, then excused me. The conflict itself seemed to take on a strange meta-quality. I wanted that day to matter somehow. I didn't want to stay the same. But I didn't want to change.

* * *

As with all research, one should question the question itself. Take the question, "Why do people need love?" Am I making assumptions about what "love" is? How does one define love? Several sources define it as putting another person's interests ahead of one's own. Does that mean that every time I grade a student's paper, I am demonstrating love? Is love just approval of some form or another? Maybe they just need me to agree with them, to ask them questions back (often, I think this is true). And if love is putting the interests of someone else ahead of yours, how do you define a person's "best interests"? Wouldn't you need to know what the "best interests" were in order to define love?

There's a feeling of love, certainly, that could be distinct from loving *actions*. I feel that feeling toward some people I don't even like. I don't like things about them, but I love them. Do I just need to feel that? Do they need me to feel it? Do they really need that kind of love?

Are there kinds of love that people need and kinds of love they don't really need?

And then, as I've pointed out, underneath that question is a question about what a person is. Are we made or do we make? When we suddenly emerge into the world are we fundamentally good, bad, or neutral? Does it change as we grow? Are we made to be good/bad/neutral or do we create the concepts of good/bad/neutral as we live?

Right about this point, I would think: I'm a writing teacher, for heaven's sake. These questions are far above my pay grade. James Berlin once commented that teaching rhetoric is to dabble in metaphysics, to argue for a "version of reality."[1] But I'm not a philosopher or a theologian, and I don't feel prepared to deal with these questions. Who does? I mean, we are talking about how to live and why to live. There's a lot at stake in how one answers.

FACTS ABOUT HYDRAS: THEY KNOW HOW MANY HEADS THEY HAVE. THEY CAN EFFING COUNT.

The panel moderator shuffled through her list of presentations. "Our next presentation will be . . . 'Facts about Hydras,' by . . . a hydra?"

---

1. James A. Berlin, "Contemporary Composition: The Major Pedagogical Theories," *College English*, Vol. 44, No. 8 (Dec. 1982), 765–777.

The hydra stood up and walked up to the moderator, who looked both curious and confused. "Yes, I'll be presenting," said the hydra. She walked up to the microphone, and cleared her throat—all three of them. "My handout is the green paper that you picked up as you came in the door," began the hydra bravely.

"You're a hydra?" asked the moderator loudly. Moderators don't like to lose control, and if they don't hear their own voices with regularity, they get very uncomfortable.

"Yes, I am," said the hydra patiently. The audience of instructors looked from their green sheet of paper up to the curious looking speaker, back down to their paper, and back up again. Some of them made immediate notes in the margins of questions that they might need to ask during the Q&A. Some checked their phones. A few whispered to each other and nodded here and there, a finger thoughtfully pressed to their lips.

"I'm sorry, but Hydra has seven or more heads," said the moderator quizzically.

"Well, yes," said the hydra, nodding all three of her heads. "But that's just in the stories. I actually only have three. I'm not hiding any extras anywhere," she said jokingly, tittering nervously, trying (but failing) to make it into a joke.

The moderator looked at her heads as if she were counting again, to make sure that she did indeed only see three.

"Our sources are very clear," the moderator said again. "Hydra has more than three heads. Now," she said, leaning toward the hydra as if she were about to tell her a secret, albeit very loudly, into a microphone, in front of an audience in a conference room, "Cerberus the hellhound does have three heads, and three heads only."

Several people laughed.

"Yes, but . . . I'm not a hellhound. I'm a hydra," said the hydra, starting to feel a little sick. The moderator sighed, and several of the audience members started to look around, bored.

"You have three heads, so you're not Hydra," stated the moderator simply. "It's a matter of definitions." She leaned forward, going into her helpful mode again. "Maybe you don't know the myths well enough yet to be sure what you are."

The hydra felt very taken aback. "But I'm trying to talk about what is real, not myths."

"Next presenter, please!" called the moderator.

The hydra felt very confused, but it suddenly seemed that no one in the room was looking at her anymore. They had all moved on to the next speaker.

The hydra went and sat down in her seat. "I heard they have excellent crepes in the hotel restaurant here," said one of the other heads, trying to cheer the hydra up.

"There was a free book of some kind in the nightstand," said the other head. "Maybe we can order crepes and wine to our room."

That evening, a member of the kitchen staff had to take a very bizarre order for room service, where three voices were simultaneously ordering crepes with a different kind of filling, and they each wanted a different wine to go with it.

CHAPTER FIVE

LESSON #5: NEVER MARRY YOUR PAPER TOPICS. BE WILLING TO GET A DIVORCE. OR BETTER YET, WHEN IT COMES TO WRITING, JUST BE PROMISCUOUS.

A big problem for students—especially those of you who have convictions, or at least you believe that being careful and deliberate with convictions is important—is that of commitment to a research topic. It seems that some of you are afraid to write a paper that argues for a line of reasoning supported by your research and evidence because you're afraid that once you've made that argument in a paper, it now has to be part of your permanent belief structure or something. You're young. What you think will change many, many times. And it should. Convictions should change somewhat over the course of your life. If you are committed to continuing to learn things and grow in your understanding of the world around you, then your convictions are guaranteed to change somewhat.

In my class, your writing and research assignments should certainly be seen as opportunities to explore your own viewpoint, but you could explore other viewpoints too. Exploring other viewpoints and trying out their arguments can, interestingly, shore up your own convictions.

For you Christians, this often seems threatening. Many of you seem to think that if I'm telling you to try out different arguments about healthcare, I must be trying to undermine your faith. I must want you to become a Satanist or something.

I kind of want you to try arguing for Satanism. I can't think of a better way to keep you from ever becoming a Satanist.

You get the point? Stop being afraid to put on someone else's glasses for a while. The fact that I want you to try to understand another way of thinking does not mean that I want you to abandon your faith. Ironically, I am convinced that trying out other ways of thinking will probably return you to your faith, with a fresh appreciation for it.

If you live your life thinking in terms of the writing lessons I always give you—dealing in terms of questions, research, validity, and reality—then I am convinced that two things will eventually happen. First, you will arrive at a relationship with Jesus. He shines in the dark, for the person who is really seeking truth, He makes himself known. Second, you won't be like many of the Christians you know.

After all, I was never much like many of the academics that I knew. Christian or not, people are not usually willing to question their beliefs that deeply.

Decide that you can develop sympathy for other perspectives without being threatened. Test the opposite viewpoint by understanding their argument. Believe that a true God can show himself.

* * *

There is no unified self, claims postmodernism. The self is fractured and contextual. Attempts at unity are important so we can stay sane, but they don't really amount to a truth or a reality that can be assumed to be stable.

In the winter of 2016, I am sitting in my office in our rural campus and looking out the window. It has been about five weeks since the Homecoming parade downtown, since the boy jumped. It is getting dark. I have just finished meeting with students to go over papers. I am tired.

I think about the papers I've gone over today and the conversations I've had. I have learned what it is like to lie in bed with a broken back; to be a single mother of twins; to see New York City for the first time; to stand in the front yard and beg your mother not to leave the family as she gets in the car with her new boyfriend; to restore a motorcycle with your best friend who will then commit suicide a month later, leaving the motorcycle to sit in your garage as a constant reminder of his friendship; to hike the Appalachian Trail on a clear, sunny day with your uncle; to be ten years old and witness your grandmother have a heart attack; to be fifteen years old and have a teacher comment about how trashy your clothes are; to visit a coffee plantation in Morocco; to adopt a child from India; to teach dance classes in a children's home; to take in a football game with a beloved father; and to pull off the most amazing Halloween prank ever.

James Berlin claims that the relationships between the

elements of rhetoric—audience, logic, and ethos—create different "worlds," evident to those who participate in the language of that world.[2] I've always said to myself that my students are each their own world, and when I try to understand them, I try to enter that world and understand its logic for itself before I try to ask them questions and get them to think about their logic or the meaning of their words.

When I read student papers, I am being instructed in my students' worlds. This means that I am being instructed on what self, truth, and authenticity mean to them. What it means to be a person. What is true. What is real.

A few months later, someone will directly ask me: "How do you define truth?" I will actually be unsure of how to answer. I will say that it's relative. To which this person will ask if anything is definitely true. I will say yes, some things are real and true. Gravity exists and is at work at this present moment. The person will ask, "Is a person's value relative?" I will say no, all persons are of equal value. And he will say, "But how can that be so, if truth is relative? If truth is relative, can't I say that some persons are of lesser value? Can't I make an argument to kill some people or to imprison some people or to rape some people?"

I will run that conversation by my colleagues and they will say that's ridiculous: Of course some things are true and of course we don't believe in killing people or raping people. I will agree with them. Of course we don't. We're all positivists, deep down.

But on what basis? When my students write their papers

---

2. Berlin, "Contemporary Composition," 765–777.

and instruct me on "What I Have Learned From _____," or "Why I Value _____," I talk to them about logic, argument, and connections between things. You need to explain why this matters: how one thing led to another, why this event caused you to ask this question, how this event provided an answer.

They are explaining a *contextual reality* to me. I don't necessarily ask them to define fundamental values like what a human being is or what life means. But their ideas about right and wrong, what is important in relationships, and their moments of insight all tell me answers to these questions. I press them to explicate those answers in writing, by clarifying what that moment on the Appalachian Trial meant, why it's meaningful to teach dance to orphans, or why they felt compelled to spend six months planning a prank.

These could all just be contextual realities that give their own lives meaning. A logos for the moment, a thread of consistent meaning that provides a framework for a student and their family.

But they all seep into me, and the ones that are joyous have elements in common, and the ones that are in pain need something that the joyous ones might have. It's not that students are only in pain or only happy, but there are connections between the happiness and the pain.

It's almost like a fractured self collecting the pieces, asserting its unity, proclaiming a reality.

There is a line of reasoning, a logic to human experience, a fundamental reality about the way human beings operate, and it is present in the earliest histories and in the papers on my desk.

In college I was often told that ways of understanding truth and reality are a result of socialization, not necessarily "truth" but a construction of the Western imagination. The Western imagination reinforces middle class values like social stability and cultural homogeneity by enforcing powerful structures that become "real." I was particularly fond of Michel Foucault and feminism; I felt that critical theory was an important part of women's liberation. I was certain that the need for critical theory and for feminist theory was all *real* and that this need made the theory *true*.

But by this point in my life, I knew that the human imagination for what is good and what is evil and what is satisfying and what is desirable transcends culture. I had studied in non-Western places, spent years in non-Western contexts, and was better read than most of my colleagues. My postmodern and feminist beliefs didn't always coincide well with my experiences, mostly because these philosophies define the human experience as a product of socialization. Yet over and over again, it seemed that something more powerful than mere social engineering was at work in human nature, human attachment, and the human capacity for love.

I look out the window at the darkening sky, the trees of the campus turning into black silhouettes. For the first time, something strikes me: I am convinced that the need for critical theory is real, because I am convinced that human beings need liberating, and critical theory purports to liberate people from the ideas and assumptions that control them. But being convinced that the *need for liberation* is real is not the same thing as being convinced that critical theory can *do the liberating.*

Fundamentally, the postmodern theories I ascribed to did not acknowledge God's existence, nor did they treat people as created beings with intrinsic, essential value. In my experience,

there was something palpably essential to the human experience, and individuals were exactly that: individuals. Because
I care about people, I wanted them to be protected and lib-
erated. But postmodern theories of protection and liberation
rejected the way that I thought of people.

I suddenly understand Jordan's irritation with the way that
university instructors describe their students: When Jordan
complained that Kenneth's description of me sounded "sanitized," he was complaining about how *utilitarian* we instructors seem to be. We talk about people like they are objects.

I realize that day, while looking over my students' papers,
that I wouldn't mind finding another model of liberation, one
that understands my students' humanity in essentialist terms:
that these kids are valuable just because they *are*.

The feeling of knowing that you are missing some important piece of truth, something you really need, can be a powerful feeling.

Why does the Bible use the metaphor of "thirst" for our
desire to know reality?

Because it's a damn good metaphor for the feeling of *I want
to understand*.

* * *

That evening I went from campus to visit Jordan at the
bar, and he decided to regale me with Army stories from
Afghanistan. While telling me his stories, he commented,
"You will never have all the information that you wish you
had when you make a decision."

"You had to make decisions under so much pressure,
though," I pointed out. "Most of us could do a better job of

having more information. Our decisions don't have as much at stake as a bunch of soldiers in a war."

"Sure. But, I mean, at some point a decision still has to be made," he said. "And who is to say which personal decisions don't really need to be made? Surely, the impact that a decision has on one person's interior life could have ripple effects on their leadership or decisions in pressured life-or-death situations."

"But when it comes to intrapersonal beliefs, there is always more information to be found," I countered. "When does a person decide that they've explored enough?"

He laughed. "They don't have to decide that they've explored enough. They just have to realize that they can make a decision without having every single piece of information possible."

I looked at him. "But how? How does one decide when one is under the impression that there are a lot of questions left unanswered?"

"It has to be personal, Kor. There has to be a personal reason to take a leap."

"Like . . . what?"

"Do people get married because they have all the requisite information about this person they are marrying? Do they know everything about this person? Have they seen that person in every possible situation?"

"No. They've seen the person in some situations. And they love them."

"Yes. So they get married. They don't have all the information, and they know it, and they take the leap."

"It's risky though. Especially with marriage. Things could change. The person you marry could change, even if you don't."

"Yes. I honestly think that choosing Jesus is less risky. He's not, you know, *moody*." Jordan looked at me pointedly.

"He could withhold important information, though," I pointed out. "Things could change based on information I don't have."

Jordan looked at me, maybe fondly or maybe with annoyance. "I wish we could have all the information we wanted before making decisions. But that's just not how life works."

The facts of my life weren't changing much: I was still teaching the same class, the same material, reading dozens of papers written by dozens of unique people, going home to my family, going downtown to take classes, sitting through meetings, and submitting my own papers. My own historical placement and exigencies were unchanged, my context was not different.

But bit by bit, my mind was being revised.

FACTS ABOUT HYDRAS: THEY CAN BE A BIT NAÏVE.

In a valiant effort to learn more about her origins, the hydra decided to visit Hades. When she arrived at his office and checked his name plate by his door, she realized that on his list of titles, he was also a dean.

"Good heavens," fussed the hydra to herself. "Why didn't I know that?" She took a deep breath and knocked on the office door.

"Come in," called Hades.

The hydra opened the door and entered the office. Hades sat at his large L-shaped desk, dressed very dean-like in a blue suit with his reading glasses in the front pocket. His office windows overlooked one of the larger campus courtyards. The hydra had the strange feeling that she had been in this office before.

"Didn't I interview you when you first applied to our department?" asked Hades, looking at her closely.

"Why, yes, you did!" said the hydra warmly, recognizing him at last.

"Make yourself at home," said Hades politely, motioning to two very comfortable looking chairs by the window. The hydra squished herself into one chair, and Hades sat down in the other.

"How are you enjoying your position here?" he asked solicitously.

"Oh, I love my position immensely," said the hydra. "I did, however, have a few questions about how I came to be here. I guess it turns out that you are a very good person to ask, since you hired me and . . . all."

Hades smiled genuinely and nodded. "So your questions are about why I hired you?"

"Well . . . not exactly," said the hydra, starting to feel a little confused. "I am more interested in the fact of my *condition*. You see . . . I'm a *hydra*." She said this leaning forward with a lowered voice and made sure he could see all three of her politely smiling heads.

Hades nodded and smiled. There was quiet while the three smiling faces looked at him meaningfully.

"Yesss?" asked Hades after a moment. "What was the question again?"

"Well, where did I come from, for starters?" said the hydra, feeling rather silly that she had not thought ahead of time and come to visit the dean with a more clearly formulated plan for gathering information.

"Hydras come from Lake Lerna," said Hades simply.

"Yes, but I mean, why does the lake, um—produce hydras? Why don't I have one head like other dragons, or why don't I have more than three? Why am I *this* way?"

Hades shrugged. "Maybe it's the water temperature. Or the level of the lake. Or maybe it's something in the sediment of the lake bed or something." He looked at her closely for a minute. "I would think three is a good number to have," he said thoughtfully.

"Well, I would rather not have three," confided the hydra to Hades.

"Well, I would like to have a Pegasus, but I don't have one," said Hades in a defeated tone. "We just can't always get what we want."

"But I'm talking about something that is part of my*self*," emphasized the hydra. "It's different than wanting to own something or wanting to experience something fun."

"Well, that's true," said Hades in a very serious way. He looked like he was really trying very hard to understand what the hydra was worried about.

"Have you ever thought that maybe you are just . . . supposed to be this way?" asked Hades in a very kind tone. "Maybe it's just a matter of accepting reality."

The hydra had certainly thought of that. She looked at Hades without saying anything.

"After all," he shrugged. "We can't really change the way we're made. You were born with three heads."

The hydra swallowed. "Yes, well. I suppose it is difficult to change the facts of one's birth," she said weakly.

Hades seemed to get fidgety in his chair.

"Did you know they've put a minibar in the faculty lounge?" he asked suddenly. "Now we can have a glass of wine in the afternoon!"

The hydras eyebrows shot up—all six of them. "Really?!" she asked enthusiastically. "That is marvelous!"

"I'll show you how to open the wine cooler in the minibar," said Hades, getting up and opening the door for the hydra. "It has a combination lock on it, of course."

"Well, of course it does!" said the hydra happily, allowing Hades to usher her out of the office and toward the lounge.

They had a leisurely afternoon talking in the lounge, and that evening when the hydra was walking down the street to her car, she saw Hades wave to her from his office window.

At home that evening, the hydra looked at her list of facts critically. "I don't know if I have anything to add, really," she said in a dejected tone.

"The combination to the wine locker is a fact," offered one head helpfully. "We could write that down."

"That is not a fact about *hydras*," said the other head.

"Well, it *sort* of is," said the other head, obviously trying to think of a reason why this was so.

The hydra ignored the bickering of the other heads and thought about her day. She picked up her green pen and wrote: *It is difficult to change the facts of one's birth.*

"That's not a fact about a hydra! You're just feeling sorry for yourself!" accused one head.

"*I'm* not feeling sorry for *my*self! I don't agree with that statement at all," sniffed the other head.

"You don't?" asked the hydra. "You *don't* think it's difficult to change the fact that I have three heads?"

"Well, no . . ." answered back the other head, suddenly unsure and shifting her eyes.

There was quiet for a moment.

"I take it back," claimed the head suddenly. "I do agree with that statement after all."

The hydra felt annoyed. She shook her head and went to find her velour pajamas.

The other two heads were much more cooperative than usual as the hydra brushed three sets of teeth for bed.

CHAPTER SIX

LESSON #6: DECISIONS HAVE TO BE MADE IN LIFE.

If you want to write a decent paper, you will have to choose a side to argue for. That doesn't mean you have to believe that particular argument for the rest of your life, but you do, at some point, have to take the plunge and make the argument. Students sometimes resist this. You want to camp out on facts and analysis and keep talking about research. But you have to get to writing the paper, where you talk about what something means. In order to say what it means, you have to get into the mindset of the facts and ask yourself questions about whether or not this research is corroborating your experiences or not.

At this point, some complaints should probably be leveled against your teacher. Like the fact that she is telling you to make a decision when it appears that she sucks at making decisions or getting to the part where she talks about what things mean to her.

One of the smarter kids I ever taught once told me, "I have no idea where you stand on anything. It's weird."

I actually think that he thought it was weird because he

felt that he was so smart he should be able to figure anyone out. In effect he was saying, "It's weird that you've managed to outsmart me, because I'm such a genius."

But I remembered that student and what he said because it caused me to realize that most people stand for something, and I had started to appear so detached and conviction-less to my students that I seemed a little "weird."

But perhaps that impulse to be detached was also the quality that made me malleable, changeable, able to take leaps and make decisions when they did, finally have to be made.

At some point, you have to jump in and write a thesis statement and run with it. You have to talk about what all the research means.

* * *

To concentrate on fact and analysis is to ignore *meaning*.

Sitting in a study room of the university library, I looked at the beige metal cart of neatly lined-up texts that were all reserved for me for the year. I had them in chronological order, and on my computer screen my thorough summaries of them were lined up across my desktop, accompanied by PDFs of important research or articles written about each one.

I had been at this all day. Day after day. It was the spring of 2017 and it had been a cold spring. My lined jacket was across the table, and I knew it was getting dark out. A thunderstorm had been promised—I could actually hear some thunder even through the library window—and I was upset with myself that I had been working all day and didn't seem to have gotten anywhere.

What was I missing? An hour before, I had flipped open

a copy of C.S. Lewis' *The Weight of Glory,* a collection of his work that one of my interviewees for my research had given me. It was my "lighter reading" for the day. In the essay "Transposition," Lewis comments that there are two aspects to understanding something: there are the facts, and there is the meaning. It is possible to be very knowledgeable and deeply analytical, but miss the meaning of something.[3] This is a lesson that I had taught you all many times, even using similar language. "But what does it *mean*?" I often ask you when you present me with a list of researched information.

Not that I always know what it means. But I know that for information to be compelling, it has to be arranged into some kind of argument that challenges something, that attempts to argue for a value. It has to answer the question "so what?"

This is a widely understood truth about communication. It's not like it should be really earth-shattering to anyone. And yet, time and again, as I have spent years of my life around really intelligent people, there is a tendency to forget this. You've probably heard older people say that throughout life you keep coming back to the same simple lessons. That is true.

I was full of facts about Christianity. I could analyze passages from early Christian treatises in terms of all kinds of things: ancient world concerns with purity of language, educational conventions of the time, and the writer's background in rhetoric.

So much information and so much analysis. And yet, what does it mean? Why does this information have value?

---

3. C.S. Lewis, *The Weight of Glory: And Other Addresses* (San Francisco: HarperOne, 2001), 113–114.

The texts looked at me from the cart. They would periodically seem creepy to me, many of their writers having been executed for their faith, and their ghosts would seem to mill around, watching me. Sometimes the ghosts seemed friendly, like they wanted to dialogue. Sometimes they seemed surly and temperamental. They were moody, like you students are.

Despite executions and exile, these writers' arguments remained. When one died, another one emerged. Fundamental Christian arguments went remarkably unchanged from the beginning of the faith to the present day. On that particular day, I was only looking at texts from the first 300 years or so, but still: These writers all believed the *same* thing. That was the thought that kept striking me.

Why is that remarkable? So men and women trained younger men and women; therefore, fundamental Christian philosophy could be remarkably consistent, right? The consistency could be located in their practices of cultural transmission, couldn't it?

What is there but facts and analysis?

Meaning.

What does it mean?

It is strange to try to relate what happened in my mind next. The closest visual I can think of is that of a gate suddenly opening. But don't imagine a pretty little garden gate. Imagine a gigantic iron gate. The kind that would be on a prison. And imagine it sliding open so suddenly and violently that it breaks.

All of these writers believed that a man who was dead had come back to life, and therefore death was no longer the end.

And they didn't just believe it the way we usually mean the word "believe." They believed it *as if they had seen it.* They were more certain of it than they were of things we generally refer to as "beliefs." They knew it was true in the way that people trust what they've seen for themselves. They would die for it—some of them happily. Because they *knew* that death wasn't the end. After all, they had seen someone come back to life.

How could they believe it as if they had seen it, when they hadn't seen it? How could they have the kind of certainty that comes from having seen something?

Because they *did see it.*

Just as a fact has one life as a series of words on the page and another life in the reader's comprehension, just as there are facts and there is meaning, there was not only a physically resurrected person, but there was a living person. These writers had seen Him. They described the same person, they were affected by Him the same way. Generations after Jesus Christ lived on earth, He was still being seen.

Of course, I am trying to describe the facts of how I came to see Him, and most of you already know that facts are part of the story, and there is an intangible quality to the reality of Him. There are words, and there is *the* Word. I thought that perhaps in this chapter I would describe how I came to believe, but naturally, now that I am here, I find that it is phenomenally difficult to do. One of the many criticisms that should probably be leveled against the writer of this book is that, in attempting to describe thoughts and why they matter, she has gotten lost in metaphors about gates and such.

But I cannot come up with much better than that for what happened that day.

A gate opened. And once opened, there was no closing it. After all, once you've seen something, you know it's true.

In the silence of that room, the meaning of the testimony of both the biblical writers and the writers of the early church was suddenly apparent and even obvious to me, visible to my mind in the sense of my reason and visible to my mind and my heart in the sense of being spiritually visible. The reason Christianity had captured the hearts of writers and "caught on" in the Roman Empire was because it was a living faith with a living God, and now that I could see that, I was totally captivated.

* * *

Walking down Parkwood toward the parking garage, the air was damp with rain that would arrive soon, and lightning was visible away in the clouds. I stood on the pavement in front of Mason Place, the thirty-five-story tower that housed our department, speckled with lighted windows in the offices where someone sat late or lights had accidentally been left on. The buildings, while so familiar, looked foreign and new this evening. The landscape of the Real had invaded my two-dimensional world, and while everything looked the same, nothing was the same. I stood on the pavement where the boy had fallen and looked up the massive tower.

What is happening to me? Am I going crazy? I'm standing on the sidewalk where a kid died, crying. This is not normal.

Everything seemed to signify new thoughts, new possibilities. I had always taken what I could see for what was Real, and now it was like I was standing up on the walls of my own perceptions, and there was something else out there. It was entrancing. It was terrifying. The something else out there was beckoning and growling, like it was hungry. But it was also Real.

If the boy had never jumped, would I be here? If Grey had never asked me why people need love, would I be here? If my brother hadn't killed himself, would I be here? If I just didn't think about things so much, would I be here? Agent of my own effing misery, I am.

Part of me wanted to go back to the room in the library, and part of me recoiled. Being in that room had just undone everything I knew. And yet, it had given me a new perspective, a new mind in a sense. Everything I knew had been undone, and there was also a sense that everything I knew was suddenly re-created. I wanted to dance, really. I wanted to cry, really.

I opted for crying, walking through campus to my car, sniffling like an idiot and wiping my nose on my sleeve.

FACTS ABOUT HYDRAS: THEY GET TIRED OF LIVING BETWEEN COMPETING NARRATIVES. SUCH EXHAUSTION CAN ONLY BE AMELIORATED BY CHOOSING ONE NARRATIVE OVER THE OTHERS.

The hydra was relaxing in the kitchen reading the morning newspaper and having morning coffee and scones when there was a loud knock at her front door.

She opened the door to find that the infernal knocker was a young man, who walked in as if he owned the place and threw a giant sword onto the hydra's sofa, with very little regard for how the point of the sword might damage any of the pillows.

"Well, we are at the part of the story where decisions have

to be made," announced the young man. "It's about like piercing your ears, I think. Not that I have pierced my ears recently, but I've heard that it makes a stinging pinch. I would guess it's going to be like that."

"Excuse me?" said the hydra. "What are you talking about?" One of the other heads said something more colorful.

"I'm Hercules, and I've brought you your sword," he said with a shrug. "So you can chop those extra heads off and get on with a normal life."

"I have to lop them off myself?! I thought you were supposed to do it!" The hydra could not believe this ridiculousness. Clearly the young man had not read the correct texts. He had no idea how he was supposed to do things.

"No one *else* can lop them off for you," said Hercules incredulously. "That's just in the stories. Please tell me you know the difference between a story and reality."

"What if I don't?"

"Well, even if you don't, it doesn't change reality. You will just have to get good with yourself."

The hydra glared at Hercules, who investigated the plate of scones with interest for a moment, but then apparently decided that scones were not adequate for his appetite.

"Well, I've done my job for now," he said, heading for the door. "I'm going to see if there's somewhere to get a decent hamburger around here."

"What?! That's it?" gasped the hydra. "That's how the story ends?"

Hercules paused. "Well, I wouldn't say anything *ends*, exactly. But that's how a hydra's heads actually get chopped off. Also, I know that my story doesn't end today, because I have several other tasks to participate in. That means that I am *destined* to find a decent burger before long, because I'm hungry and I *have* to get my other errands done."

"This is ridiculous," fumed the hydra. "I will *not* accept this situation. I can, after all, determine the ending for myself. Self-determination. Personal agency, and all of that."

Hercules shrugged. "Okay. I mean, I guess you can pretend I never dropped the sword off. But, I mean, even if you pretend, the sword is still *there*." He made a dramatic teenage motion toward the desecrated sofa.

The hydra huffed and smoke swirled around her head.

Hercules shut the door unnecessarily hard as he went out. A few pictures clinked against the wall, and the china in the cabinet rattled.

The hydra picked up her coffee mug and threw herself down in her favorite reading chair. She lifted the mug to her lips. Three heads went for the lip of the mug at the same time, slammed against each other, and the cup was dropped. It shattered across the floor, coffee spattering all over the hydra's legs.

"Oh my God, I am so tired of this!" wailed the hydra and began dramatically sobbing.

"*What* did she say?" snorted the second head nastily to the third, which rolled its eyes and gave an enormous smoke-filled sigh.

The hydra suddenly stopped sobbing. She sat and thought. The sword glinted knowingly on the sofa.

The second and third heads got *very* quiet.

One might say they looked wary.

CHAPTER SEVEN

LESSON #7: REMEMBER PATHOS. KEEP YOUR AUDIENCE IN MIND. WHEN POSSIBLE, MAKE THEM LAUGH.

When writing instructors say "pathos," they are referring to your audience connection. You should always keep in mind that you are a fallible human being, speaking to other fallible human beings. If you keep that in mind, you're more likely to approach your audience out of concern rather than irritation, and you're more likely to speak with humility rather than arrogance.

Even though you're a student, don't disregard the importance of treating your instructor-audience with sympathy. You probably don't realize that, despite age and life-stage differences, your teachers do learn from you. I don't mean that we "learn" from you in terms of facts and information. Most of the time, we're ahead of you in those areas, because we're older and we've studied more. But what we learn in our interactions with you has to do with the heart, with the intrapersonal self, with who we are as people. We learn both from the process of teaching you, and from our relationships with you. Age and experience count for some things, but they don't count for everything.

You've heard people say that parenting is hard, that they had to die to themselves, that sort of thing? Teaching is related to parenting in the sense that the teacher has to have the maturity to bend down to the level of the student, to put their perspective aside enough in order to enter the perspective of the student, all in an effort to help them progress.

Being a writing teacher creates a strange dynamic, because while I am your audience for your papers, I'm trying to get you to think about and imagine other "audiences," and while I try to teach you about "real-life audiences," you are my audience. Communication doesn't happen without an audience. And once there's an audience, something is being communicated, whether we are aware of it or not.

This whole process of teaching and entering other perspectives is instructional for us teachers, but we also learn from seeing how you students respond to us. I notice when my students like arguing with me, agreeing with me, talking to me, or are willing to make me laugh. I notice when they loathe me, too.

* * *

Christian students get really bent out of shape about abortion. They care about it a lot. This is something I noticed from my first semester teaching. Any time I assign research papers or ask students to write an opinion piece or something persuasive, several of the Christians will pick abortion.

During the 2016–2017 semesters, I taught one of the brighter kids I ever had, a young man named Aaron. Aaron was very quiet, sat in the front, listened to everything, rarely spoke in class, and then would come to my office and ask very hard, insightful questions. He was far ahead of his peers as far as his maturity and attitude toward people, and this conflicted with the lack of actual experience that came with being a young kid from a family whose social world centered around a small church. Unlike some of my other students, I failed to realize while I had him just how much he was challenging me and how much I was learning from him. I taught him while I was wrestling seriously with my own identity as a Christian and an instructor, and he wasn't a loud or brash student, so he slipped under my radar. It wasn't until he was gone that I realized how much he had affected me and how he had unknowingly led me into several quiet insights about teaching.

Predictably, Aaron wrote a major paper about abortion. He announced in my office that he wanted very much to be able to persuade a pro-choice person of the validity of the pro-life viewpoint, and he wanted me to help him. He had always been very open with me about being a Christian, but at the same time he didn't generally resort to citing the Bible for everything. So, as he laid out his research plans for me and told me of his intentions for this project, I couldn't resist asking him some questions.

"Why do Christian students get so worked up about abortion? I mean, why is it a huge deal to them?"

"Because it's murder," he answered simply.

I just looked at him. "I know that you believe that," I said, "but really, why are Christian students so invested in it?"

"Because it's murder," he said, almost laughing. "Why

wouldn't we get worked up about it?"

I stared at him. "I already understand the argument that it's murder," I said. "But what I'm asking is, why do you care so much about it?" (Yes, I actually asked him that, in just that way.)

Aaron looked like he might get mad. "Because it's murder. Who doesn't care about murder?" He glared at me. "And who can't understand that murder would be a 'big deal'?"

"I care a lot about murder," I said defensively. "I am just trying to figure out why so many of my Christians want to write about abortion, above anything else, when given a choice of topics. I think it's just because it's something you guys are raised discussing . . . well, it's a set of arguments that your whole community takes very seriously."

"That might be true," said Aaron. "I take it you're from a different kind of community?"

I explained that my thoughts about abortion were that every abortion isn't equal. Just because you're killing cells doesn't mean you're killing a human being. Of course the cells are alive from the beginning of conception, but that doesn't mean they're a conscious, living, separate being. At some point, they are alive like my finger is alive and part of my body but not a separate self.

"Like your finger?" asked Aaron, seemingly confused.

"Yeah, you know. Or my hand," I said holding up my hand and wiggling the fingers. "My hand is alive. Living cells. But we don't call my hand a human being, it's an extension of me and my body."

Aaron seemed to be studying my hand for several seconds, like he was really considering my black nail polish or something. Then he took out his phone.

"Let's play a game," he said.

"Um, okay?" I said.

"You like to write. You always write back to my emails," he said.

"Yeah, I think well when I write."

"Okay, I'm going to write you an email today. Respond to it. The way you want to respond, the way you naturally would."

"Um, okay," I laughed.

An hour later I got an email from Aaron: *My girlfriend is pregnant. We just found out. We are definitely going to keep this baby.*

I sat back. Was his girlfriend really pregnant? Was the discussion about abortion upsetting? Or were they considering an abortion? I felt sad. Maybe he felt like our discussion was taking away from his happiness at becoming a father. I thought Aaron would make a great father.

I thought about all these worries and feelings crashing together and then decided to stop being codependent and just answer as myself.

So I wrote: *Aaron, I know you're young to have a baby, but I'm excited for you and your girlfriend. Being a parent is a beautiful thing. . . . PS: Is this email real? Are you really going to be a dad? Because I really meant everything I just said.*

Aaron wrote back: *Thank you for your reply. You're really awesome. I'll send you another email in a second.*

I was perplexed.

Email #2 came: *My girlfriend has a hand.*

An hour later he wrote: I'm waiting for your reply.

I wrote: *Congratulations?*

He wrote: *Wow, that's a really different reaction from the news that we are going to have a baby.*

I wrote: *Wow, you're really annoying me. Are you going to have a baby or not?*

He wrote: *You're really interested in whether or not I'm going to be a dad but not really interested in my girlfriend's hand?*

I wrote: *Now I know you're making the pregnancy up. You're just trying to make a point.*

He wrote: *Trying?*

I wrote: *I see that you didn't like my fetus/hand analogy. It's still a good analogy—I was trying to point out that a fetus isn't conscious like a person. So it's different.*

He wrote: *But a baby isn't conscious the same way an adult is. So is it okay to kill a baby?*

I wrote: *No.*

He wrote: *A baby is a potential grown-up, and a fetus is a potential baby. How do you decide when it's okay/not okay to kill it?*

I wrote: *Is your girlfriend really pregnant?*

He wrote: *I wish!*

Aaron's sense of humor about our differences was always enjoyable. I didn't meet many students—or their families in our community—that were willing to try to build a sense of camaraderie with me through humor.

* * *

Aaron is in my office, waiting while I read a draft of a paper. He's writing about the history of his hometown, trying to connect memories with stories of how certain city structures were built. It's quite clever.

I'm looking down at the paper and reading slowly, making marks here and there for places I want to comment on, but I can feel Aaron looking around my office, assessing and analyzing. If we are talking, he always looks directly at me, but since I'm "busy" with his draft, he feels free to inspect the room. I can feel his curiosity and his desire to learn more about me.

I have one family picture out. My husband and I, our children squished between us, with mountains in the background. Aaron leans toward the picture, closely assessing—what? The places we vacation? The fact that we hike? Trying to guess where we are? The way my spouse's arm lies around my shoulders? The way my kids grin goofily? There are quite a few things that could be learned from this picture, I realize. I'm wearing a t-shirt with my undergraduate alma mater emblazoned on it; my husband's ball cap has his hometown sports team on it. My children are clearly tiny versions of us.

Aaron is smiling and he almost asks a question once or twice but then stops.

Finally: "You have two kids, Mrs. Kori?"

I look up, smiling, pretending I just suddenly realized that the picture has his attention.

* * *

An Interlude: I am in Chicago one year earlier. An editor I had worked with happened to be there, so I emailed him. He suggested lunch. I said yes.

Lunch was wonderful, but the air was heavy with overtones; he had expectations and wishes that hung in the air. It wasn't that he adored me personally; he was lonely, and insightful women can be very appealing to lonely men.

In an Uber on the way back to the hotel where I was

staying, he tried to touch my hand. Tried, but I moved it, acting like I needed to adjust my bag by my feet. I didn't like him, but even if I had, this is how I think: I think of all the people that would not know, that would never guess, that mean so much to me. I have this perverse belief that it matters when I maintain my integrity, because I care about these people. My family certainly, but I think about my students, my colleagues, and the graduate students that wander through my office to discuss recipes and Trump and their disastrous love lives. I want them to have a Kori who doesn't have secrets.

As I got out of the Uber, he said, "You're a good woman."

"I'm a well-behaved one," I conceded with a wink.

He smiled, pleased that I was willing to let him off the hook without recrimination.

The interlude is over, but I could write another one and another one and another one, if I wanted.

Which, I don't.

The point is, these interludes happen.

* * *

Back to my office with Aaron, I smile and tell him my children's names, my husband's name, what he does for a living.

I can answer his questions cheerfully because I have no weight on my conscience, and I want him to receive images of family from a woman with a clear conscience. From a Kori who, even if she is effing clueless in many ways, can at least demonstrate fidelity toward family.

Aaron watches my face when I talk about my family and asks questions about how I met my husband.

"You want a family, don't you?" I ask him.

"Yes," he nods. "I do, sometime. Want to be a dad."

"You'll be a good father. I can tell."

He smiles, looks away, turns a little pink. He is glowing.

His glow makes my heart glow. I go back to studying his paper and start to point out to him where he is supporting his thesis effectively and where the paper is weak.

* * *

I have this bizarre conviction that these interactions count and are possible because I keep a clear conscience. That in some way the behavior my students cannot see does matter.

But it's the year that I have Aaron, the young man who stated so clearly he wanted to be a dad, who so obviously admired my husband's place as the leader of a family in that photo, that I realize that this is a form of love. Keeping my ethos intact while I am their teacher is a way of loving them.

On the last day of class that semester, Aaron wrote me an email telling me how much he had enjoyed the class. I sat in my office for a long time after reading it, looking at my Marvel posters and dozens of books on rhetoric, reaching, writing, and argumentation. I thought about how my love for my students had led me to believe that I should maintain my integrity, my character, my ethos. Now my love for my students was leading me to ask questions about how to love them as a Christian. I couldn't see the way forward to an identity as a Christian instructor. I was tempted to give up, to stop trying to figure out how my public teaching practices should change as a result of my new personal identity. But whenever I thought about my students, I found that I could not stop asking myself questions; in fact, I could not stop thinking about it. I couldn't let the issue die just because it was scary or difficult to answer. And I realized again: that is love, too. Because I love them, I will keep growing.

I have no idea if my students ever think about these things.

CHAPTER EIGHT

LESSON #8: REMEMBER ETHOS. FIGURE OUT WHAT COUNTS AS CREDIBILITY TO YOUR AUDIENCE. THEN DECIDE IF YOU CARE.

When writing instructors talk about "ethos," they are talking about your character and credibility as the writer. "Credibility" is actually subjective, and so is "character." Both notions are dependent upon other people's perception of you and their worldview. This really bothers those of you who like the notion of an immovable ethical standard by which you may judge the character of others. I understand why you're bothered by the idea of a proliferating number of ways to judge character and credibility. However, you cannot force others to understand credibility or character from a Christian standpoint. You are going to have to work within the constraints of reality, which means that you are dealing with people who do not see things the way you do.

So how do you project credibility to an audience that may have different ideas about credibility? There's two important things to think about here. The first one is that you need to have a clear idea of who your audience is. You do have to figure out who you are going to talk to, in a piece of writing. Are you talking to other Christians? Members of your church? Other students? Your classmates? Your instructor? When you have a choice of audiences, you need to think about the audience that will respond to your ethos. You might need to adjust your presentation of your ideas, so that your audience will understand better.

The second thing you have to realize is that in order for your ethos to remain intact, you have to know who the hell you are: What do you care about, and why? What are your values and how do they shape your perceptions, and what do you want out of your experiences and interactions with people (including the things you write)? You might feel like you're young and that's way above your pay grade, and that's fine. But you're not too young to think about the importance of ethos or character, and to realize that confidence in your identity is what guides you through choosing audiences and choosing how to project credibility to them, even if they misjudge you, misinterpret you, or discount you. Paul is a great study in an ethos that flexed with his moods and the different audiences he wrote to: he could be loving and patient like a Zen master, and he could be pissed off and give orders like a drill sergeant. That's because he knew exactly what mattered to him, how much it mattered to him, and what he wanted from his audience. His character remained intact regardless of how he felt.

I know this isn't a simple concept, and in fact it's something that you will never "finish" dealing with. Every day of your life, you will get up and do something or communicate something in some kind of setting where you have to make these kind of decisions:

—How much are you willing to flex your values for an audience? Which values are most flexible and which are least flexible?

—Whom do you consider credible and why? How does this affect your own ways of demonstrating your credibility and character to those around you?

—What does it mean when someone rejects your ideas? What does it mean about them and what does it mean about you?

—What are you willing to do to protect your image as a Christian? What kind of commitments and rules do you make in an effort to protect that image? When do those "rules" help you protect/project and honor the character that you are trying to develop, and when do they contravene your values?

In class, we apply these ideas to your presentation of your research, but in fact they are questions that matter every day in everything you do. The way you answer the questions won't always be the same in every context, but you should always be able to think about these questions and why your answers might be changing. Your answers to these questions will alter your career, your family life, and your relationship with yourself.

* * *

One of the difficult features of my journey into the Christian life was the extreme loneliness. Part of it was the result of the fact that I lived between worlds. I knew a lot about Christianity, lived my life around Christians, and then taught and worked and had friendships with people that had no contact with the Christians that I knew. I could fit in anywhere, but didn't feel particularly known or connected anywhere. I have several personal idiosyncrasies that incline me toward solitude—I'm extremely introverted and my preferred activities are reading and writing—and these qualities only heightened the degree to which I felt alone in my journey.

Moving from one worldview to another is not instantaneous, and one of the features of my spiritual journey was how many steps—and how much time—was spent figuring out how to move from one way of thinking to another. The notion that there is a process is somehow threatening to many Christian believers, as if the fact that people don't change instantly invalidates their conversion or means it wasn't powerful enough. Difficulty with process and change is a feature of many people, not just Christians: the human mind seems to like categories, to like the idea that we can quantify everything and everyone around us. It's difficult to work with the idea of being "between" categories, but that's what a process is: someone learns something and slowly changes. From the moment I stood on the corner of Parkwood and re-recognized the entire world around me, I was grappling with some sort of perplexing and tiring question. Everything from "What does this mean for how I will parent my kids?" to "Am I going crazy? Am I just hearing things and I think it's my 'heart' or some such nonsense? Is a 'heart' just a constructed notion so that I can hide behind it and claim that Jesus is talking to me?"

For me, this process of learning and transitioning was exacerbated by the public/private divide that teaching imposed on me. It's possible for a person to have two very different "lives": the one they live at home with their family, and the one they have at work. You each realize that you can be one person at home, and another around your friends. Some of this compartmentalization can't be avoided, and this is normal. You can be the same person in two different environments but use different language to express yourself or do different activities. You can adjust your ethos while still reflecting the same set of beliefs.

I had, at some point, adopted a very laissez-faire approach to philosophical questions about meaning and God, and that was fairly consistent across my personal and public realms. But once it became important to me to communicate something consistent and meaningful to students, that started to fracture. As I worked out my personal beliefs in the safe environment of my private life, and as I grew in my faith, it was difficult to translate that into my work life, where research projects and syllabi that I had put in motion long before were now creating friction.

I also found myself wedged between kinds of Christians: there are churches aplenty in my community, and the few families that had connected to me and taken an interest in me were all very different. And then there was, I knew, somewhere out there, an academic community of Christians. As in, people who were not in seminaries but were practitioners of the Christian faith and taught in English departments just like me.

I went in search of a Christian academic community. There were very few public Christians who were publishing and teaching as Christians in my field. Somehow or other, I decided that I must find My People. This would help me to grow, to figure out who I wanted to be as a Christian teacher. I needed people who would help me learn How to Do This Christian Professor Thing.

Predictably, this led to some mishaps. I could tell countless stories here, and some of them are very funny. But I'll stick to the ones that I think speak most clearly to the problem of compartmentalization for teachers. After all, I was consistently motivated along this journey as a result of my desire to be the best teacher I could be for each of you.

* * *

In 2017, I attended a national conference where a group of Christian professors were scheduled for a panel discussion about Christian faith commitments and the teaching profession. I don't actually remember the precise title of the panel, but it was the main thing that I was looking forward to that year at the conference.

I sat in the audience, waiting for the presentation to start, feeling very happy. I wanted to hear how other Christians articulated their spot in an academic field largely dominated by postmodern thinking, identity politics, and materialist philosophies.

As they started to talk, each of the presenters identified themselves as part of a different Christian denomination. This was a sign of inclusivity on their part, as a community. Which, inclusivity is usually a good thing, in my book. I loved the idea that all of us, while from such different backgrounds, were connected by our belief in the same God. We had all had our library moment.

As they continued to talk, it seemed that part of the point of the discussion was, in fact, inclusivity. How inclusive their Christian philosophy really was, how closely it aligned with the academic arguments and epistemologies of their colleagues, of other panels being presented there at the conference, of all their mentors, of all their students.

The discussion was punctuated with statements and arguments that were fundamentally materialist. While some of the discussion aligned with Scripture, some of it diverged in important ways.

I deflated slowly. If that seems funny, well, in hindsight my naiveté is pretty funny.

Now, if you are one of my jaded Christian students, you will make comments about how you are not surprised, and how the professoriate sucks and how this is what's wrong with the country and such. If you are one of my liberal Christians, you will think I am being too conservative and exclusionary, and if you are one of my conservative Christians you will start arguing with me that none of these people on the panel are "real" Christians.

All of your arguments miss the point. The problem, my dears, is that all of these people are real and they are Christians. And in this public moment where they had the chance to identify as Christians and define Christianity for a room full of public intellectuals, it sounded an awful lot like Christianity was so eternally inclusive that it was meaningless. It had nothing specific to offer to instructors who wanted to make a difference for their students, or for students who were thinking about jumping from a window.

Each of you (and you know who you are) sitting in my office at various moments over the years did a better job of representing the faith. You might be young and lack experience, and really bad at being gracious sometimes, and I might have been rude to you, or I might have been patient, depending on the day. But you each did a better job of presenting your beliefs in a consistent way that honored the unique message of the faith, than these people did.

But I digress.

In the conference, I sit and watch the postmodern Christians (who definitely exist) discuss their way through political views, teaching justice in the classroom, and the need for a revised history of Christianity in scholarship. They talk for an hour. The whole time, I'm hunting through this pile of discourse and looking for my own entrance into their world.

But I don't want what they are offering. They don't sound any different than I was before the night on Parkwood when I re-recognized the world. While it is painful to change, I don't want to go back.

But one thing you can say is a fact about Kori: I don't give up when I should.

I approached one of the women on the panel and asked for a private conversation that afternoon. We met in the hotel coffee shop, and I told her my story and pleaded my case.

"I'm struggling to figure out what it looks like to be a Christian and an academic," I explained. "I am trying to figure out how to integrate these identities in a way that is meaningful, that serves my students well and is genuine, that portrays God well to those around me."

"Do you consider yourself a *Christian teacher*, or do you consider yourself *a teacher who is a Christian*?" she asked me.

I knew the distinction she was making.

"I have to be a Christian teacher, I think," I explained to her. "Being a teacher who happens to embrace Christianity puts spirituality in the back seat to my teaching practice, and I don't think I can do that. Actually, I don't think I have ever done that. I think that my notions of spirituality have always been the basis for how I taught. It's just that since embracing Christianity, I am more aware of it." Then I made a big mistake. "I think that Christianity has given me a larger picture of my discipline than the other worldviews, and a richer understanding of teaching as an intellectual transaction. But I don't have anyone else to talk to about these issues, and I need a community that will help me."

Her eyes glazed over, and her eyebrows were perfectly still. "I don't consider myself a Christian first. I consider myself a person and a teacher first. Christianity is the spirituality that I think is most open-minded and loving, that I choose to integrate into my worldview."

This woman was kind and gracious with her time that morning, but was also quite clearly not interested in investing any additional energy in me if I was going to insist on a "Christian teacher" identity as opposed to being "a teacher who happens to be a Christian."

Back in my hotel room, I lie down on the bed and try to shake out my mind. I understand the way the panel members think. I understand *why* they are reasoning the way they are. But it is weak reasoning, to claim the faith and its text, and then reject elements of the text that one doesn't like. They don't appear to have a hermeneutical stance that strives for any consistency, and there is no explanation of how they rationalize a Christianity built on postmodern assumptions about reality and knowledge.

Bad apologetics, I whisper to myself, and wonder where I learned that term. I've never heard myself say such a thing. I must have made that phrase up.

I feel a lot of compassion for academics that try to straddle worlds the way these panel members did: If one is a Christian, someone who works in a field where thinking practices and social norms push back against Christian belief, it is not a wrong impulse to look for ways to ameliorate the pressure and connect one's Christian identity with one's academic identity. It's normal to seek ways to connect one's public and private identity into a cohesive self.

Except these people haven't actually connected their identities. Their public and private selves are coexisting in a state of uncomfortable juxtaposition, where in one moment one identity is dominant and in the next moment the other identity is dominant. This isn't integration of identities, it's compartmentalization.

I don't like it, I say to myself while lying on the hotel bed, in my petulant internal voice that seems to be reserved for conferences. I don't like being different people at different times, I don't like the feeling of inauthenticity when my public and private worlds brush up against each other only to start fighting each other. I also don't like that in such exchanges, it is inevitable that one identity is subsumed by the other. Part of me often feels cheated, wronged, and irritated. I want to feel whole, and I want who I am to mean something.

I certainly didn't solve the problem of public/private compartmentalization right there while lying on the hotel bed. But it was an important moment in my journey, because I recognized a few things to be simultaneously true: That to be a "Christian teacher" doesn't mean that one locates specific points in a curriculum where Christianity can be inserted, nor does it mean that I simply take my curriculum to a "Christian school" and teach writing in an institution where I've signed a doctrinal statement. The problem of compartmentalization is created by the fact that two ways of thinking are clashing; to focus on curricular questions is to miss the point. It is not possible to "integrate" postmodern thinking, a curriculum that values materialist assumptions about reality, and a Christian identity in a consistent way; at least, not in the way that I wanted my teaching to be meaningful. The problem was not how to make my public and private selves overlap so that they didn't argue with each other, and it wasn't how to find "balance" between two separate worlds. The problem was how to let my private self—the part that wanted to be like Jesus— become my public self, too. That couldn't be achieved by following a list of "Christian teacher dos and don'ts." It could only be achieved by giving control of everything I did and believed and valued over to Jesus, a process which had slowly been happening since the day in the library.

Strangely, I wished for a moment that I could ask Grey if he had ever thought about this, if this didn't speak to some of his confusion about whether or not he was "saved." *I should write him a letter*, I thought.

I did start a letter that day. It would get to be 80 pages long before I would realize what I was actually trying to write about . . . and that I was actually writing to *several* people.

Now, this will sound like I made it up, but I didn't: In a breakout session the next morning, the woman I had had coffee with was sitting in front of me. She didn't realize that I was behind her as she described our conversation to a colleague of hers. "I mean, it was like I had been asked out *on a date,*" she said with dismay. "All those personal questions!"

I am not sure why, but this made me very angry. It was like I was standing on someone's front porch, holding flowers, knowing for certain that the people in the house know I'm here but will not open the door.

The rest of my time at that conference was spent with my usual non-Christian friends: Jenny, my feminist friend who also loved sci-fi, and my friend Roger. With both of them I was able to text, get coffee, or ask personal questions without it being *like a date.* (And exactly how a "date-like" coffee meeting is offensive, I'm still not sure.) Plus, the two of them were often focused on some of the same questions that concerned me: What is the real meaning of everything we are doing here? Is this really going to help our students? Why can't hotels get comfortable seats for conferences, anyway?

When the speakers were at their most boring, we would sit in the last row and create detailed rating systems for how numb our rear ends were. We figured that we always encouraged our students to use quantitative data in their papers, so we should certainly model the responsible use of data.

* * *

A few weeks later, I sat in an office at another university, having a conversation with a Christian professor who had written a wonderful book about curricular design. I had asked him to look over my course objectives and even my dissertation proposal. Research proposals require that researchers disclose their philosophical background, and the proposal I had written reflected the difficulty I was having finding language that honored my faith and was comprehensible to my colleagues. At one point in the conversation, this man seemed to feel some exasperation as he waved his hands over my work and said, "There's no such thing as a postmodern Christian."

I pointed out some of my phrases that I had chosen, the ones I felt were problematic, and explained, "I am very influenced by postmodern theory, and I am a Christian. I haven't necessarily found language I'm comfortable with that reflects who I am *now*. I'm working on that. I am still talking and writing some in my old way, while I am growing and trying to find new ways." I thought my admission of being a person in process would elicit some thoughts about his own process or recommendations about what to read and who to talk to.

Unfortunately, he repeated himself: "There's no such thing as a postmodern Christian. Christians turn to the Bible for their answers, and the Bible does not support any of the answers found in postmodern social theory."

"I love the Bible. I think it's awesome. I believe what you're saying. But the thing is, I still think like a relativist much of the time, and a social constructionist some of the time. I am growing, but I haven't figured everything out yet. I am a very postmodern-thinking *Christian*."

He just shook his head.

I was speechless. I wasn't sure how I could make it any clearer. I was sitting there in front of him, explaining myself with reasonable clarity, and he simply insisted that I didn't exist.

Later, on my drive home, it occurred to me that I had just argued with someone about whether or not I was a *real* Christian. I still laugh to myself when I think about that.

* * *

The postmodern Christians at the conference were Christians, but I wasn't going to fit in with them. They were not the academic community I had been hoping for. Christians who came from more fundamentalist backgrounds were Christians and couldn't comprehend me—to them I was a fake, a postmodern variety of believer that wasn't "real," someone they couldn't relate to. Both communities were happy to exclude me, but by now I knew I was looking for something different anyway. I would just have to be patient and let God lead me to a community.

* * *

I have a suspicion that the peculiar experience of being on the outside of my own faith is probably not isolated to me. The precise conflicts that are present in these two stories—conflicts between perception and truth, perception and reality, insiders and outsiders, and tradition and historical exigency—have consistently emerged and re-emerged in other experiences I've had and in the experiences of my peers. I have no doubt that you could add your own illustrative stories. Academia isn't the only place where Christians have to make hard choices, and it's not the only place where they have trouble with credibility and consistency, but it's the context that I know best and that I can use as illustration.

If these experiences were morality tales, the moral was that I needed more clarity about who I was and who I wanted to be. Being a Christian doesn't solve all of a person's identity problems, and relying on how other Christians perceive the world is not always helpful. We cannot forget that ethos is partly constructed from our assumptions, and we shouldn't confuse those assumptions with reality, nor should we assume that we can change the way others make assumptions about us. Years later, I am still working on these same problems, albeit in new ways. As with most things in my life, I tend to make discoveries in a weirdly deductive, trial-and-error sort of way.

FACTS ABOUT HYDRAS: NOT ALL HYDRAS ARE ALIKE.

The hydra paused, straightened her jacket, adjusted her glasses, took a deep breath, and rang the doorbell. *Be brave,* she told herself, as the door swung open.

A very smiley hydra was at the door, inviting her in. This was a meeting of hydras, and the hydra was very excited to find out how other hydras dealt with being hydras. I mean, it gets exhausting to listen to so many voices and viewpoints, and how does one ever make decisions this way? The hydra was hoping for some guidance.

Over the next hour, she met several hydras, but all of them were strange. One of them had 20 heads, and the hydra could not hold a conversation with him. Another one claimed to be a Marxist hydra and talked about the labor of hydras. He seemed to think the topic was very romantic, but the hydra felt that it was boring and kind of missed the point. Then there was a regular human man there who kept insisting he was a hydra, when he clearly was not. Still another one was a hydra pastor who kept reassuring the hydra that he understood her situation and that she could relax and be herself here. While it was very kind of him to be reassuring, the hydra did not feel relaxed.

Back at home and freshly bathed, the hydra got out her notebook to write. The fact that there were other hydras had not improved her spirits about being a hydra or about living life with extra voices around her all the time. The hydra wrote, *Fact: the existence of other hydras is not in and of itself a reason to feel pleasure or pride that one is a hydra.* She thought about it for a few minutes. Then she wrote, *Fact: A group that demonstrates the reality of a principle is not a proof either for or against the correctness of the principle.*

"The fact that there are other hydras just means that hydras exist; it does not tell us whether it is good or bad to be a hydra," she mused to herself. She pursed her lips unhappily. "That's a bit philosophical for a hydra," she muttered to herself. "A bit above my paygrade."

So she wrote, *One should not join a group just to have friends,* because that seemed simpler.

Then she wrote, *One should not join a group just to feel a sense of belonging,* because that seemed even better.

Then why should one ever go to a party? she wondered. "One should go to parties if one believes in the principle of the party. And only then should one go," said the hydra to herself.

"Have we settled anything?" asked one of the heads, waking up.

"What is all this nonsense about parties? I dislike parties immensely," sniffed the other head.

"We were at a party this evening and you did fine," argued the hydra.

"That's because I ignored everyone," said the head.

"You were eating the whole time!" accused the other head.

"There is one thing we didn't consider," mused the hydra. "What if one believes in the principle of the party but doesn't care for anyone who is *at* the party?"

"That's a dumb question," announced one head. "We never have that problem!"

"Just go to a different party," said the other head, exasperated. "Why go someplace where they've confused their principles and their parties?"

The hydra thought for a minute. "Well, what if they haven't confused their principles, but they're just not very nice?"

One head snorted and blew her bangs out of her eyes. "Sounds like they are a waste of time. And what kind of principles do they have if they're not very nice?"

"That's a good point," admitted the hydra. "I might write that one down." But she didn't, because secretly she suspected that that head was missing the point.

"I guess you have to think about how much comfort you would sacrifice for the principle," said the other head.

The hydra looked at that head. "That's a very, very good point," she said approvingly and wrote down: *Which is more important, the principle or the people at the party?*

All the heads looked at that question in silence for a moment.

"Is that a fact about a hydra? I mean, does that belong on the list?" asked one head.

"Yes," said the hydra breathlessly. "Yes, I think it's a very important fact."

"It's not a fact, it's a question!" One head was getting fussy and quarrelsome.

"A question can point to a fact," answered the hydra serenely. She went into the kitchen and put the teapot on, much to the approval of the non-quarrelsome head.

"Questions don't point to facts," grumbled the other head.

"No amount of tea is going to answer the question for you."

"Earl Grey or the rooibos?" the hydra pertly asked the other head, pointedly ignoring the first head's discouraging comments.

"I'll have what you're having," the other head said in an attempt at camaraderie. "After all, we should try to have a pleasant party amongst ourselves, even if we have no clear principles."

"*We have principles!*" roared the first head.

The hydra was put out. She felt she *did* have principles, but the head that was roaring about it was really making it hard to think.

"We'll have the rooibos," she said curtly and poured the water while looking straight ahead, ignoring both of her constant companions.

CHAPTER NINE

LESSON #9: ALWAYS DEFINE YOUR TERMS.

How you define terms like "knowledge" or "truth" or "reality" determines what you think you know and what you can actually write about. I've told you several times that you don't, right now at age 18, have to have a definitive answer to these questions about how to define important terms, but you do have to be aware that the definition changes the discussion. If you don't know that, then other people—your friends, your family, your instructors—will seem incomprehensible to you. You will wonder how on earth someone could think ____, or what is wrong with people who don't think ___? If you realize that these differences are sometimes best explored by explicating what you can know about something and how you know it, then you will have more clarity surrounding all the inevitable conflicts of your life.

You don't necessarily start your papers with a detailed explanation of what you think about knowledge and how you came to make the argument you make in the paper. But I can actually tell what you think "knowing" is based on the kind

of papers you write and the statements you make in class. Students are always identifying what they think is "good" or "bad," and those two terms alone reveal a lot about the person using them.

If you think about this with your instructors, you will understand why they sometimes discount your arguments or why they don't get your humor. Sometimes you're just not very clever or funny. But sometimes the problem is that the two of you look for knowledge in completely different places.

* * *

The day before the spring semester of 2017, Roger and I were drinking coffee, eating cookies, and playing chess in one of the faculty lounges. I'm not a very good chess player, but I like to play chess and teach my friends. It is a fact that there are now several mediocre chess players in English departments around the South, thanks to me.

On this particular day, Roger and I got onto the topic of memorable students.

"Did you ever have Kevin?" I asked, around a mouthful of chocolate chip cookie.

Roger almost sneered. "Oh my god, yes. I had him. Difficult kid."

I chewed slowly. "He's difficult. But I liked that kid."

Roger rolled his eyes. "He was good friends with Chase, that other kid who came from the same school."

Oh yeah. I remembered Chase, too. He was "difficult" as well. He once wrote me the note that said, *I object to the strong language you use in this class.* I told Roger about that note. "I had only used the words crap and shit," I explained. "It's not like I was using really bad words."

"That story doesn't surprise me," said Roger. The amount of disdain in his voice surprised me. "They complained about a movie I assigned, because there's a scene where a girl is half naked." I looked at Roger thoughtfully. Something about this conversation was bothering me. It wasn't the words; it was the tone. Roger sounded unusually nasty.

Then Kathryn came up, a girl we had both taught. "I asked her what she thought about the class," said Roger, "and she asked me if I really wanted to know, and I said yes. So then she says, 'I think you're the mouthpiece of Satan.'" Roger was clearly very pissed off about this. His voice rose a little as he repeated her statement, and he snorted cookie crumbs in my direction.

I giggled and choked on my cookie. "That's funny, Roger," I said.

"It is not!" he said, indignant. "What gives some student the right to say something like that to me? How is that constructive or even rational?"

"It's not, really," I conceded. "But you asked an eighteen-year-old girl for her real thoughts. And she gave them to you. You can't really take it all that personally. I would just be curious why she thought that."

"Well, I'm not curious," said Roger. "I don't care why she thinks that. She obviously was taught to think that and doesn't want to grow up. She would rather just parrot what her parents think."

"In her mind, she is growing up. She is growing up into her parents. And her parents probably have more tact than she does," I said thoughtfully. Roger grunted and moved a chess piece. We played in silence for a few minutes (except for the sound of our chewing) while I thought through my reaction to hearing this story about Kathryn. After a few minutes I realized that I was actually a little *envious*. I liked Kathryn. I wished she would have been as blunt with me about her thoughts.

"You know, I'm a little jealous, Roger. She said something she really, really thought. They rarely do that. They rarely say what they really think of us. It's kind of a privilege to hear it. Granted, it's a privilege in a very backhanded way and all, and I wish she didn't think that about you, because I don't think you're the mouthpiece of Satan and all. But it's kind of cool that she was willing to say her real thoughts."

Roger shoved his chair back and looked at me with undisguised disgust. The chess game was apparently forgotten. "You're making excuses for two things: backward ways of thinking and poor manners. That's what she has, and you're excusing both of them."

"I'm not excusing her parents for telling her that her teachers are Satan's minions," I protested. "I'm not excusing her for choosing her words poorly. But I cut her some slack for thinking it, because she's super young and doesn't know much about what she thinks yet, and I give her a few props for bravery and transparency. Come on, surely you can see my perspective about that."

"I don't."

"You asked her what she thought. You gave her permission to say her thoughts, and she said them."

Roger shook his head and looked at me almost sadly. "Who are you? There is no reason to defend her."

"I'm not defending her, Roger. I'm trying to encourage you to see the situation in a more balanced light. She's eighteen, for heaven's sake. What eighteen-year-old girls say is not some-thing to get upset about."

Roger stood up slowly. Went to rinse his mug out in the sink.

"You know, kids like that come from families that wouldn't defend us if we said our 'real thoughts,'" he says, his voice sounding strange and squashed. "They don't care about our perspective, or your perspective."

I'm stayed very quiet and very still. "I know," I said. I felt terrible.

"They don't care about anyone else's perspective. Ten years from now, they won't care about you or what you taught . . . or that you tried to accommodate their back-assward beliefs."

"I know," I said again. I *did* know.

"And it's not helping anyone for you to try to see their side, either. You're not doing them a favor. You're not doing your-self a favor."

Roger left the room. The faculty lounge on that floor is win-dowless, with fake plants lined up on a bookshelf that contains old anthologies, and a hard-working Keurig on the counter flanked by several quasi-clean coffee mugs.

Fact about Roger: His frustration with me sprang from the fact that he fundamentally cared about me. To him, I was slip-ping away somehow, wandering into territory that threatened to harm me. One of the few instructors I knew who frequently allowed himself to feel paternal affection toward his students, Kathryn's words were a blow, because he had opened him-self up to her and she had acted in bad faith by going on the attack. A Christian who would undoubtedly have fumed with anger if she heard herself characterized as "anti-intellectual" or "back-assward" for her faith, it apparently didn't bother her to characterize instructors as "satanic."

Fact about me: I am an expert at depersonalizing the kinds of comments Kathryn makes. To me they are an object of intellectual interest. It is hard for students to actually hurt my feelings in a personal way. Also, bravery in young people endears them to me, and so the guts involved in standing up to a teacher is often a way around my defenses.

But I was spooked by the fact that I cared about Kathryn's viewpoint. I was also spooked by the fact that I could imagine seeing the world in the good versus evil terms that she did. What could be happening to me, that I would actually make space in my heart for a student to claim that there was something wrong with what Roger was teaching? That I would make space for a student's rudeness, for a student's willingness to say something unimaginable . . . to accuse us of having chosen the wrong side, to be acting from mistaken impulses, when clearly we all had chosen to be there out of a desire to do good?

I also wondered if my overall openness to the opinions of young people was a terrible character flaw. If Roger had taught Grey, what would have happened? Would they ever have had the discussions that Grey had with me? Probably not. If Roger had had Aaron, would Aaron have announced a desire to change Roger's mind about abortion? Probably not. Why was I open to these kids? Why did they talk to me about this kind of stuff in the first place?

A conversation with Grey played in my mind, from sometime in 2014 when I didn't know him very well. He had written something about the concepts of "good" and "evil" and how there was not a satisfactory distinction between them in some essay I had assigned. I did not think it was a very good paper. The reasoning was fuzzy, and it wasn't really clear how he defined good and evil. So I asked him.

Me: "So, obviously here you believe in good and evil but I can't see what your logic is for either of them."

Grey: "Everyone believes in good and evil."

Me: "No, they don't. Some of us believe that's a matter of perception, or motives."

Grey: "That is a perspective that allows a lot of evil to occur."

Me: "But what 'evil' is depends on how you define good, and people define it very differently."

Grey: "Yes. That's why it's important to define it correctly."

Me (exasperated): "But there are different ways of defining it."

Grey: "There's different ways of defining a lot of things. That doesn't mean that every way of defining it is correct."

Me: "Sorry, I got off track there. What I mean is that you need to clarify how you define it, here in this paper."

Grey: "But if I do that, you'll tell me to use other sources. That makes it hard."

Me (super exasperated): "Then use the Bible, but qualify your argument as being from your perspective, from a Christian perspective."

Grey (glaring): "Okay."

Issues of good and evil abound in my conversations with students. To write well, you have to know what you think about something, and being able to figure out basic things like good and bad and right and wrong are the basis of thinking clearly. That fact alone was always difficult for a relativist like me, and I was having a harder and harder time keeping up the relativist part of my teaching ethos.

Sitting there, staring at the fake plants and the Keurig, I realized that something else had changed: I no longer believed we were only doing good. I was open to Kathryn's accusation because, fundamentally, I was plagued by a feeling—and quite a few thoughts—that something was wrong. There were divides in the teaching world, and they aligned themselves along the fault lines of relativism and the belief that good and evil could be defined, *should* be defined, and that arguments and knowledge arose from those definitions. I had become convinced that the progressive philosophies on which my classroom had been based were mistaken, that the moral relativism I strived to embody as an instructor was wrong, and that, worse yet, it encouraged students to embrace a hopeless perspective that offered no buffer against things like jumping out of windows.

Do I have to pick a side? I asked myself. *What will that mean for my life? For my profession? For my friendship with Roger, one of my favorite people?*

I stared at the chessboard, specifically at the little cedar queen. I could imagine her looking up at me and speaking in the teacher voice I often used in class. "Of course you don't have to pick a side," she seemed to say. "Unless, of course, there is an objective you want to achieve. If you want to win at something, you must choose a side and play to win. So the question is, do you have an objective? Is there something you want to win?"

The answer to that is easy: My objective is to be a good

teacher. I want to win my students' minds to something that is good for them.

"Well, then," tsked the queen. "You have something you want to win. You will have to choose a side that you think achieves your objective, and then you'll have to play from that side."

I was a little depressed for the rest of that day. A feature of my conversion that is difficult to describe is the way that my thinking had to change, gradually, over time. To re-recognize the world as having a living God is only the first in a myriad of steps that meant I often sat back and wondered who I was and how to actually *be myself* (meaning, Kori-as-she-thinks-and-reasons-now), given that I had a track record of being *someone else* (Kori-who-thinks-and-reasons-some-other-way). Sometimes I would look back at myself and think that I had actually been fairly clear-thinking in my earlier beliefs, and sometimes I would think about old conversations or things I had written and I would realize: *Daaaang, I couldn't reason my way out of a paper bag.* My sense of reality had changed that much.

While looking at the fake plants and talking to the chessboard, I realized that I had reached a point where the conflict between who I had been and who I was and who I wanted to be was reaching a painful point because I now had new ways of defining things. I realized that my ideas of good and bad were never going to reverse themselves and, more critically, they were always going to separate me from my colleagues in some way.

A few days later, I received a phone call from a previous student who was studying engineering in Colorado. He needed a copy of the syllabus from my course in order to get transfer credits, and I emailed it to him while we chatted on the phone.

"What did I teach you that is actually useful in your writing assignments?" I asked him while sending the email. That's a question I always ask previous students. Beware, if you run into me in a parking lot or call me for a syllabus, I am going to ask you this.

"What you know depends on your sources," was the thing he said had stuck with him and served him well. "It gets me away from talking about what I *think*," he said. "I stick to what I can say I *know*, given my sources."

After getting off the phone I thought about the word "knowing." How do we know things, and where does real knowledge come from? I had taught this student that he could only know what his sources demonstrated, but what about the sources themselves? Why credit some sources and not others?

In 2013, I would have said that knowledge was almost entirely constructed, including truth itself. Knowledge begins with personal experience, historical exigence, and social engineering. This statement is partly true: What we think of as bodies of subject-area knowledge are dependent to some degree on experience. But I had extrapolated from this that fundamental reality itself—the presence of any knowable truth—was dependent on experience.

In early 2016, I would have said, "I don't effing know," which was probably a better place for me to be than earlier, and it would have certainly elicited complaints about my use of language from some of my students.

In early 2017, I would have said, "Don't tell anyone, but I'm thinking that we cannot know anything apart from what we have been led to know." And I would have left it at that.

Which is a tad vague.

By the end of 2017, I had run aground on the issue of defining knowledge. I had sat and stared at plastic plants while talking to a chessboard.

I was avoiding the truth that all knowledge begins with God. This is a truth that still took me a few more weeks to articulate out loud. This particular definition upended all my prior experience. It upends the current intellectual milieu of the university, as it creates a fundamental rift between those that want to be Christian instructors and those instructors who just happen to be Christian.

I would never have tried to use my faith to make an academic argument of any kind though. I didn't know how. When I asked myself why I didn't know how to do that, it seemed that all the answers pointed to the depth of the differences between a faith-based way of knowing (we call this "epistemology") and the empirical way of knowing that was accepted at the university. It is one thing to understand that these are important distinctions. It is another thing to realize *how* important.

If you understand this issue about defining the beginning of knowledge, then, as a student, you will understand more about what is going on around you in a university setting than your peers. As I've explained to some of you in class, you don't have to be a Christian in order for the importance of this question to greatly enlighten your ability to perceive, understand, and interact with the people around you.

During this time, I spent a few weeks trying to write a new kind of text for my class. I took all of my old material and tried to collate it according to the same rhetorical principles I often taught from, but I also tried to rewrite all the introductions and explanatory material from my new perspective. I wasn't necessarily trying to write a book that I would actually use. It was more an exercise in figuring out how Christianity might be relevant to my teaching, a way of re-examining the core logic of both writing-as-a-discipline ("discipline" meaning "subject in school") and the core principles of my course.

There was a point where I was particularly frustrated with this exercise. It seemed that I was trying to force together internal monologues that couldn't recognize each other. Writing is generally a good way to integrate my thoughts, but I often felt that I was trying to explain how I knew that something was true, when it *couldn't* be true. Like trying to argue that something mythical was real, that I had just seen a hydra get in her car and drive down the road, or something else equally ridiculous.

Except I *knew* it was real. And *knowing* that had changed everything.

At some point during this period of frustration, it occurred to me that while I often thought of Christianity as being something that people privately take on "blind faith" and the world of disciplinary knowledge as something we teach based on what we see, the truth was that faith isn't blind. It is a different kind of sight. I could choose to see my discipline through my new sight. It was possible, it turned out, to live a holistic life by always beginning with God as the source of knowledge and thinking about disciplinary knowledge from that standpoint. It took practice, and it still takes practice. I still have days where I talk to plants and chessboards.

In hindsight, part of why this transition took a while is that I had to get comfortable with mourning losses. Conversations like the one I had with Roger had to become something I was more comfortable with and better at handling. For whatever reason, Christians often think that conversion makes relational choices obvious and easy, that our web of pre-Christ relationships is simple to alter, and that it doesn't grieve someone in long-lasting ways to change the way they relate to the people who have stood by them. In reality, I had to take small steps and experience the cost in incremental ways that taught me to trust a Savior who knew more than I could ever learn.

CHAPTER TEN

LESSON #10: MAKE SURE THAT YOUR CONCLUSION ANSWERS THE QUESTION "SO WHAT?"

Students often think that it's self-evident why something is important. But it never is. You need to point out what is so pressing about your topic that you were compelled to write about it.

This is where you really have to make a distinction between analysis and meaning. For example: I can see that you wear the same t-shirt several times a week. The shirt is worn and has a hole in the shoulder, but you persist in wearing it. The t-shirt must be important to you or represent something important. That is description and analysis.

Meaning, on the other hand, answers the question "So what?" It describes the significance of the t-shirt. From my standpoint, the t-shirt might be significant because it is from a concert, and I make some assumptions about you based on the fact that you seem to like that music. From your standpoint, the t-shirt might be significant because it's your brother's t-shirt and he is away at school and you miss him. Or maybe you hate the shirt, but you don't have a money for a new one, and you resent that people think you like this music.

I once had a student who was a future engineer and he kept writing about newer and better light bulbs. How they worked, how much more efficient they were in terms of energy and in terms of cost. I asked him, "Why should I care about these lightbulbs? You've written a report on lightbulbs, but have not answered the 'So what?' question."

"They're cheaper and more efficient, that's why you should care," he said.

"No, those are facts about the lightbulbs. And they're encouraging facts," I explained. "But why should I want to read ten pages about electronics?"

My student was visibly annoyed. He actually snatched the paper from me. "People are just too lazy to make changes that would be better for everyone," he said pointedly. In his opinion, I was obviously just too lazy to understand that I should go home and change the lightbulbs in my house. But his irritation with me had revealed one reason he actually cared about lightbulbs and one reason he might actually be able to persuade me to care: The lightbulbs represented something communal to him, both a communal ignorance toward better options and a belief that saving energy was a way of helping others. Now there was a compelling significance that he could tie the topic of lightbulbs to.

You do have to spend time talking about the t-shirt or talking about the lightbulb. Certainly you need to make us understand what the shirt looks like, how big the hole is, and so on. Certainly, explaining wattage and giving us a chart of costs will help us to get the idea of just what "efficiency" means when it comes to lightbulbs.

But don't forget to close the argument by coming back to your topic's primary significance. This primary significance should have to do with people. When you write, you are communicating something about yourself and the world. So be sure that I can tell why you wanted to communicate this to me.

* * *

"A million things could have happened in the ancient world that would make people think someone had come back to life. And you're telling me that Christianity caught on because somebody *actually* came back to life?" Kenneth's eyes were bright. He was annoyed.

Now, I had not said that Jesus came back to life. Don't give me credit for bravery or something. I had just been explaining that there wasn't a good explanation for the emergence of Christianity. Specifically, we had been talking about how converts to Christianity were convinced that death was no longer the end. They had a new reality. This was a strange way for a new faith to emerge from Judaism. At least, I thought so. Kenneth wasn't that impressed.

"Martyrdom was a means to an end, perhaps. A rhetorical statement," he argued.

"These were regular people, though," I pointed out. "I don't think they would have been planning mass suicide as martyrs for a yet-unestablished belief system."

Kenneth rolled his eyes. "I mean, how many people are we actually even talking about? A few people being killed could

Dr. Ryan K. Strader

be recorded as if it was a lot of people. How can we even know that it was actually a significant number of people?"

(In the back of my mind, I could hear Aaron asking me, *Who doesn't understand that murder is a big deal?*)

After talking around the history for an hour, Kenneth sighed and folded his hands on his desk. Then he said something that caught me off guard: "I have never believed. I wish I had what it took to believe."

"I'm not sure what 'it' is, but I don't have it either," I said. "I'm always confused and second-guessing myself. It gives me a headache, sometimes."

"You do have it. You do. You might be totally fucked up right now, but you have it." We sat in silence for several seconds, then he sat back in his chair and said, "No one is going to hire you except a seminary."

That hurt, because it meant he wouldn't vouch for me at any of the institutions that I had wanted to teach at. He was cutting me loose from his network.

"A seminary definitely does not want me," I said. "I am hardly competent to teach as a professional Christian."

"Well, then. You are just totally fucked."

I wasn't sure what to say, so I just held my hands up and shrugged.

"It doesn't bother you, though," observed Kenneth.

"Not too much. I am convinced that I am going to be okay," I said. I meant it. I couldn't imagine what might happen or not happen to me, but I was sure that I would be taken care of.

* * *

A few weeks later, I went to a lecture given at a church on

the northeast side of the city. The speaker had written a text on apologetics that I had liked, and I heard he was delivering a short presentation on a Saturday afternoon at a friend's church.

The church itself was very formal and traditional, with curved pews and lovely blue carpet in the sanctuary. I skirted around the back pews, trying to figure out where I would want to sit, where other people wouldn't block my view. As I was casing out my possible vantage points, I saw a glass room at the back of the church. There were racks of books in the window.

It was a bookstore! In a church! So cool! I looked through the window. So many books! My little bibliophile heart went pitter pat. I couldn't help but speed up as I got to door, turned the handle, and, as I moved to go through the door—I actually ran into the door. Like, flat against the door. Because it had not opened when I thought it had. Because it was locked. Like, the bookstore was *locked*.

Also, I had spilled some coffee on the carpet when I ran into the door. I had to go find paper towels to clean it up. There were a few people giving me strange looks while I did this, like they couldn't imagine why I would try to blot my coffee out of their nice carpet.

I decided to sit with the other college instructors—there were a few that I recognized from two other universities in the city. We chatted and got along well. I mentioned the coffee and the paper towels and the bookstore.

"You're not supposed to have drinks in here," someone explained. "There's a sign where we came in."

Oh. No books, and no coffee. Criminy. "No wonder there's not many academics here," I joked.

One guy pursed his lips and looked around, assessing. "There's quite a few of us, really," he said thoughtfully.

Aw, he didn't catch that I was joking about the books and the coffee. These were definitely my people: even while they are yearning for books and coffee, they are socially awkward and don't get my humor about the lack of books and coffee.

The speaker was quite good. With a lovely swath of white hair that moved when he spoke, and a slight accent that I recognize as marking him as being from the same place my family is from, he paced a bit when he spoke and used marvelous illustrations.

"Worldviews are often described as lenses," he said. "But really, they are more like cities that we live our lives in. The skyline of the city becomes the shape that we take for granted in the sky, and the city walls block out our view of the landscapes beyond."[4]

I was captivated by this analogy of the city. You students know that I'm taken with it, because I use it too often in class.

The part of the city picture that stays with me is was the fact that I am so tiny within a city. Thinking of that metaphor brings to mind walking down the main street through the urban campus downtown, the towers that comprise our academic buildings rising over me, and beyond those towers are other tall buildings housing the rest of the city, other universities, a host of global companies. I am just over five feet tall. I am swallowed by my city, both literally and figuratively.

Outside of the city, I think of the little campus where I

---

4. Os Guinness, *Fool's Talk: Recovering the Art of Christian Persuasion* (Downers Grove, IL: InterVarsity Press, 2015), 238.

teach all you crazy kids. We walk outside and see trees, a narrow road that leads to the grocery store. Out here we don't have a sky blocked by towers, but by multitudes of churches and middle-class box stores. Most of you were born here, and this skyline is all you know.

Back in that moment, sitting in the church, I looked around at the groups of churchgoers, people who obviously considered this their "home" church. Not one of them had a coffee mug in their hand, and none of them were trying to barge into the bookstore. They were well aware that no drinks were allowed in the sanctuary and that the posted hours for the bookstore were Sunday, from noon to 2:00 p.m. They already knew the rules. They also seemed to know each other, to be happy together.

I wondered if any of them have been in any of the buildings familiar to me and what they thought about the experience.

* * *

From inside the cities of the other worldviews, Christianity is incomprehensible. From inside the city of Christianity, the other worldviews are irrational: they don't hold together with any compelling logic. But people believe things because it makes sense to them. To those that believe in them, postmodern philosophies and relativism feel more loving, inclusive, and generous. To those that believe in them, materialist philosophies seem more truthful, just, and reasonable.

What is inexplicable at first for those of us who move from one city to another is that the Christian worldview is exponentially richer and deeper in its capacity for reason, love, and truthfulness about the world around us. It's only inexplicable at first, though, as we figure out what our choices mean: those who come to Christ experience an increase in their capacity to reason, because knowledge begins with God.

That doesn't mean it's fun or easy to change the way one thinks. It's a difficult first step just to acknowledge that one does in fact live inside of a worldview and that the ideological spires of that worldview's cityscape might be in the way of seeing other places, other landscapes. It's another difficult step to get up on the city wall and spy out other territories. There's a serious problem for anyone who wants to visit the Christians over in the other city, because some of the citizens over there will start hollering about postmodern Christians.

It's no surprise that some academics would rather just eat one of their own heads than deal with all of this. I suppose for some of us, the internal bickering just gets too loud and we have to go on a walk through the desert, away from all the cities, to figure it out. This amounts to seeing that our city is confining us, and it's a moment in our lives where our intellectual geography is perforated enough that the truth might intervene. C.S. Lewis once used an interesting metaphor about life apart from Christ, which he said was like a two-dimensional picture. The mistake we make is that we think two-dimensional pictures "sprout out into real trees and grass." What actually happens is that "real landscapes enter into pictures."[5]

* * *

---

5. C.S. Lewis, "Transposition," in *The Weight of Glory*, 112.

This will seem like it can't be true, but it is: just before defending my dissertation, I received an email from Grey, the prickly kid who, four years earlier, had asked me why people need love. He had gone off to a state school and was doing well. "I was just wondering how you're doing, and what you're writing," he said.

Now, how should I answer that question? I wondered. Exactly what do I say to these students, when I bump into them in the campus coffee shop or when they write me an email, and ask, "How are you? What are you up to? What are you studying? What are you writing?"

"You just *tell* them," said Jordan in an exasperated tone. "It's not a difficult question."

"It's difficult if the answer is a years-long story about figuring out what to believe."

"Well, don't tell them *all* of that. Find a way to summarize it, and make it sound more normal."

"I'll never write any of them back if I have to tell my story in a *normal* way. If I tell anyone any of this, it is not going to sound normal."

Jordan rolled his eyes. "You think you're more unusual than you are. Just pretend you're writing a letter. Write it out so you can see how to make it more succinct."

"A letter. About my classroom. And all these years of teaching them and thinking about what they said?" I asked, simultaneously intrigued with the idea and a little overwhelmed. How would I fit all of that into a letter?

"Yes. Write that letter. I'll look at it and tell you how *bad* it is." Jordan smiled with the same herculean audacity of all the students I've loved.

"Okay," I said. I went home and sat with my computer. *How*

could I tell this story? I asked myself. No effing idea.

I looked at my bookshelf. I have shelves of books from different periods of my life, from different perspectives, from all of the different ideological cities I have lived in. I have loved so many different kinds of books, different kinds of ideas. I thought about how different ideas had led me to be different Koris at various times and how the pressure of teaching had pushed me toward finding a more consistent Kori who was most interested in the ideas of Jesus.

A small dragon wearing a smart brown jacket walked in with a tray of coffee items and placed them on my desk. "I was told to bring you coffee, not tea," she said in an explanatory tone. "I do hope I chose correctly."

"Well, yes you did," I said. "Thank you very much." I fixed myself a cup of coffee while the dragon perused my bookshelves with interest.

"I have many of the same books," she said. "Isn't that interesting?"

"Fascinating," I said, looking her up and down. She adjusted her glasses and jacket, and I saw that there were bandages peeking out from under the collar.

"You're a very strange metaphor for a letter to my students," I said.

"Yes, well, I suppose that is a complaint that will be lodged against you," she observed. "But, you know, I'm also a strangely *accurate* metaphor," she claimed with a pert expression. "Did you know I used to have *three* heads and not *one*?" she asked.

"Well *yes*, I did know that." I answered.

"Oh," the hydra sighed with great relief. "It is such a pleasure to meet someone who *knows* about hydras!"

"Would you like to stay while I write?" I asked. "It's always nice to have company."

"Oh, I would love it! I'll just relax right here and read a book on . . . well, hmm. So many books, it will really be very challenging to decide which one to read today." She looked at me apologetically. "Decision-making is not really my forte."

"Yes, I know," I said in what I hoped was a very understanding tone. "Take your time. I'll just be over here writing."

"Oh, *thank* you," said the relieved hydra. She turned back to my bookshelves and I turned back to my computer screen.

Facts about Hydras, I typed. Below that, I typed: *1. Hydras are real.*

I looked up from my screen. "I'll be accused of proselytizing, of trying to get students to believe that Jesus is real and Christianity is true," I complained to the hydra.

"Yes, well. We can't really avoid people having objections to things that are real. That is still another *one* of the *many* complaints that will be lodged against this book," said the hydra. "I think we should just write it, anyway," she said in a conspiratorial whisper. Although, even a dragon's whisper is still quite loud.

"Naturally, you are correct," I said graciously. Then I turned back to my screen and continued writing.

ACKNOWLEDGMENTS

It is not possible to acknowledge everyone who has played a part in the journey of writing this little book. Thank you to Jennifer for modeling the writer's life and George for teaching me about audience. Thank you to Dave and Mike for insuring that some of the chapters had more philosophical clarity. Thank you, Larry, for providing the right kind of publishing outlet (the kind that allows hydras to publish) and Gail for sensitive copy editing. Great thanks to all of my past students, especially Daniel, Shelby, and Alex, my original "research subjects." Thank you to Peter for asking me how I define truth, Justin for dropping everything to baptize me, Andy for redefining "Christian" at a critical moment, and Ken for believing in the vocation of teaching. Niki, Amanda, and Beth, thank you for being my closest friends, and for making sure I have adventures away from my desk. Clive and Os, thank you for writing the books that helped me write in dark times. My kids, Quinn and Elijah, are to be greatly admired for the patience they show toward their writer mom. The greatest thanks of all go to my partner and best friend, Joel. Since we met, he has protected my time and my heart so that I can teach and write without hindrance.

www.ingramcontent.com/pod-product-compliance
Lightning Source LLC
Chambersburg PA
CBHW071134200626
46817CB00018B/2978